PASSION AND
THE PRINCE

PASSION AND THE PRINCE

BY

PENNY JORDAN

First published in Great Britain 2011
by Mills & Boon, an imprint of Harlequin (UK) Limited.
Large Print edition 2011
Harlequin (UK) Limited, Eton House,
18-24 Paradise Road, Richmond, Surrey TW9 1SR

© Penny Jordan 2011

ISBN: 978 0 263 22232 6

Harlequin (UK) policy is to use papers that are natural,
renewable and recyclable products and made from
wood grown in sustainable forests. The logging and
manufacturing process conform to the legal environmental
regulations of the country of origin.

Printed and bound in Great Britain
by CPI Antony Rowe, Chippenham, Wiltshire

CHAPTER ONE

LIFTING her head from her camera, through which she had been studying a model posing provocatively in matching bra and briefs, Lily recoiled instinctively from the scene in front of her.

Almost naked male and female models—the girls all fragile limbs and pouting mouths, some of them open in conversation, or drinking water through straws so as not to spoil their carefully applied make-up, and the boys with their gym-toned bodies—stood together as they submitted themselves to the attentions of hovering hair and make-up artists. Fingers tapped away on mobile phones, gleaming tanned skin contrasted with the catalogue client's underwear all the models were wearing for the shoot. Heavy beat music boomed out into the small space despite the fact that some of the models were listening to their own iPods.

In other words it was a normal chaotic studio fashion shoot.

'Has that last male model arrived yet?' she asked the hairstylist, who shook her head.

'Well, we can't hold the shoot any longer. We've only got the studio for today. We'll have to use one of the other male models twice.'

'I can spray on some dye that will darken the blond guy's hair, if you like?' the stylist offered, reaching out to steady the rail containing more underwear to be modelled as it swayed danger- ously when one of the models pushed past it.

Looking around, Lily felt her heart sink. She had grown up in this world—until she had turned her back on it and walked away—and now she disliked, almost hated it, and all that it repre- sented.

Given free choice, this cramped, shabby studio with its familiar smell—a mix of male phero- mones, sweat, female anxiety, cigarettes and illegal substances that seemed to hang invisibly in the air—was the last place she wanted to be.

Edging past a chattering group of models to get to the door, she put down her camera on a nearby table and went to check the pose of the pretty girl with the wary charcoal-grey-eyed gaze, wondering as she did so how many young hopefuls had entered the industry imagining that they would leave with a contract to model in a top fashion magazine only to discover a much seamier side to modelling. Too many.

This kind of shoot was the unglamorous rump end of what it meant to work in fashion, and a world away from money-no-object glossy magazine shoots.

She hadn't wanted to do this. She was here in Milan for a very different purpose. But she had never been able to resist her younger half-brother's pleas for help and he knew it. Rick's mother—her father's second wife—had been very kind to her when she had been young, and she felt that it was her duty now to repay that kindness by helping her half-brother. She couldn't ignore her sense of duty any more than she could ignore all their late father had been.

She had tried her hardest to dissuade Rick from following in their famous and louche father's footsteps, but to no avail. Rick had been determined to become a fashion photographer.

Satisfied with the model's pose, she went back to the camera—only to frown in irritation as the door to the studio swung open, throwing an unwanted shadow across her shot, along with an equally unwanted suit clad male torso. The missing male model had obviously finally arrived—and ruined her shot by stepping into it.

Thoroughly exasperated, she pushed back the shiny swing of her blonde hair and told him, without removing her gaze from her camera, 'You're late—and you're in my shot.'

It was the sudden silence and the stillness that had fallen over the rest of the room that alerted her to the fact that something was wrong. Her senses picked up on it and reacted by sending a quiverful of tiny darts of anxiety skimming along her spine. She stepped back from the camera and looked up—right into the coldly hostile gaze of the man who had just walked in. A tall, dark-haired, broad-shouldered, expensively suited man, whose body language reinforced the same cold hostility she could see in his eyes along with proud disdain. Against her will Lily could feel her eyes widening as she took in the reality of the man confronting her, her pulse beating unsteadily against her skin.

Whoever this man was, he was obviously no model. Even stripped he would be... He would be magnificent, Lily acknowledged, her stomach suddenly hollowing out with a sensation that took her completely off guard. If asked, she would have said—and meant it—that she was inured to male good looks, and that as far as she was concerned sexual attraction was a cruel deceit on the part of Mother Nature, designed to ensure the continuation of the species and best avoided. She had grown up in a world in which beauty and good looks were commodities to be ruthlessly traded and abused, which was why her own beauty was something she chose to downplay.

She intended to be crisp, cool and in control as she queried, 'Yes?' But instead of the apology for ruining her shot and the explanation of his presence she was expecting, she received an even more hostile look of silent, angry contempt that raked her from head to toe.

As yet he hadn't so much as given a sideways look at the scantily clad girls who were now, Lily saw after a look at them herself, all gazing at him. And no wonder, she admitted.

He made the young male models look like the mere boys they were, for all their muscles, but then he *was* extraordinarily handsome—handsome, but cold. And Lily suspected judgemental. He exuded an air of raw male pride and sensual power, even if there was a grim harshness about his expression that warned her that whatever had brought him here it wasn't going to be good news—for someone. But not her. He couldn't be here for her, so why did his presence have every one of her carefully rigged inner alarm systems breaking into a cacophony of warning?

She was her parents' daughter, Lily reminded herself. At some level that had to mean she was as vulnerable to that kind of overpowering male sensuality as her mother had been. And just as capable of using her own beauty for commercial exploitation? Lily struggled to repress the feeling that made her shudder—as though against an unwanted male touch. She would *never* allow herself to repeat her mother's mistakes.

She was here to do a job, she reminded herself, not to give in to her own insecurities.

Whatever had brought him here to this shabby studio it wasn't the prospect of modelling work. His face might be as commanding and as harshly delineated that a hundred thousand ancient Roman coins might have been struck in its patrician and imposing image. It might be the kind of face that could lead vast armies of men into war and entice any number of women into bed. But it was a face that currently bore an expression of such cutting contempt that if it was captured on camera it was more likely to send prospective buyers running for cover than rushing out to buy what he was supposed to be modelling.

Was he going to say anything to break the pool of tense silence he had created?

Lily took a deep breath, and repeated determinedly, 'Yes?'

Another ice-cold look. The man must be close to inhuman, removed from the emotional vulnerabilities that affected the rest of the human race, not to be affected by the tension she could almost feel humming on the air.

'You are the one responsible for this?'

His voice was quieter than she had expected, but redolent with the same power as his presence and grimly harsh.

Lily gave the studio and the models a brief concerned glance. He was obviously here on a hostile mission of complaint of some kind, and since she was standing in for her half-brother she knew that she was obliged to agree.

'Yes.'

'There's something I want to say to you—in private.'

A rustle of reaction ran through the room. Lily wanted to tell him that there was nothing he could possibly have to say to her, and certainly not in private, but there was a nagging suspicion at the back of her mind that her half-brother might have done something to provoke this man's anger.

'Very well,' she conceded. 'But you will have to make whatever you want to say brief. As you can see, I'm in the middle of a shoot.'

The look of blistering contempt he gave her made Lily take a step back from him, before reluctantly moving forward through the door he was holding open for her. Out of old-fashioned good manners, or more in the manner of a guard determined not to allow his prisoner to escape?

The studio was in an old building, its door sturdy enough to block out the speculative questions Lily knew would be being asked by all the models and stylists inside it. She stood on the small landing at the top of the stairs that led to the studio, keeping as close to the door as she could.

At such close quarters to him there was nowhere to escape to—he was blocking her exit via the stairs by standing next to them.

'Call me old-fashioned and sexist,' he told her, 'but somehow finding that it is a *woman* who is procuring young flesh for others and profiting financially by doing so is even more abhorrent and repellent than a man doing the same thing. And you *are* such a woman, aren't you? You are a woman who lives off the vanity and foolishness of others, feeding them with false hope and empty dreams.'

Lily stared at him in disbelief. Revulsion filled her at the accusation he had made, accompanied by shock that he should have made it. The thought crossed her mind that he might be some kind of deranged madman—only to be squashed by the message from her senses that this was a man who was perfectly sane.

She pushed her hand into her hair a habitual gesture of insecurity and told him shakily, 'I don't know what all this is about, but I think you must have made a mistake.'

'You're a photographer who seeks out vulnerable young idiots with the promise of a glamorous modelling career that you know is all too likely to destroy them.'

'That's not true,' Lily defended herself, but her voice wobbled slightly as she made the denial. After all, wasn't what he was saying really very much in line with the way she herself felt about the modelling industry?

She took a deep breath, intending to tell him that, but before she could do so he continued grimly. 'Have you no sense of shame? No compunction or guilt about what you do?'

Guilt. Ah, that was the word above all others that could trigger off an avalanche of dark memories inside her—a word like a poisoned dart aimed at her unprotected emotions. She had to get away from him, but she couldn't. She was trapped here with him on the tiny landing. In her mind's eye she saw the panic he was causing in her manifesting itself into a wild flight to escape from him, a desire to curl herself up into a ball of flesh so small that it could not be seen—or touched. But that was just in her imagination. The reality was that she could not escape.

'This world into which you are attempting to drag Pietro—my nephew—is one of cruelty and corruption in which young flesh is used and abused by those who crave its beauty for their own debauched purposes.'

His nephew? Lily's heart was thumping wildly. Every word he said carved a fresh wound into her own emotions, lacerating the too thin layer of fragility that was all she had to protect them.

'I have no idea how many young people have fallen victim to your promises of fame and fortune, but I can tell you this. My nephew will not be one of them. Thank goodness he had the good sense to tell his family how he had been approached with promises of modelling work and money.'

Lily's mouth had gone dry. She had always particularly disliked this aspect of her father's work, knowing what painful fires of experience young models could be drawn into by the unscrupulous. To be accused as she was being accused now was such a shock that it robbed her of the ability to defend herself.

'Here's your money back.' The man was slamming down a wad of euros. 'Blood money—flesh money… How many of the vilest sort of predators were you planning to introduce him to at this party you invited him to attend with you after the shoot? Don't bother to answer. Let me guess. As many of them as you could. Because that is what this business is about, isn't it?'

Rick had invited the young man to accompany him to a party? Lily's heart sank even further. Rick was a sociable guy. It was normal for him to go out after shoots and have a drink. Besides, it was fashion week, and Milan was full of important people from the top of the fashion tree. It was also full of those at the bottom of that world, though. The kind who…

She could feel a shudder of revulsion gripping her as her skin turned clammy with remembered fear and her heart pounded. She wanted to breathe fresh air. She wanted to escape from the past this man and their surroundings had brought back to her.

'People like you disgust me. Outwardly you may possess the kind of beauty that stops men in the street, but all that beauty does is cloak your inner corruption.'

She had to get some fresh air. If she didn't she was going to pass out. Think of something else, Lily told herself. Think of the present, not the past. Focus on something else.

The effort of trying to refocus her thoughts caused her to sway slightly on her feet. Immediately he came towards her, taking hold of her to steady her. Her brain knew the truth, but her body was reacting to a very different message that had her demanding with fierce anguish, 'Don't touch me.' Her reaction to being imprisoned was instinctive and immediate, ripped from deep within her as she panicked and used her free hand to try and prise his fingers away from her wrist. But all he did was drag her further into his imprisoning hold.

Crushed against his body, Lily waited for the familiar feelings of nausea and terror to flood through her, but instead—unbelievably, and surely impossibly—her senses were sending her messages of an awareness of her captor so unfamiliar to her that they stunned her into a bewildered stillness.

Could it really be happening that, instead of filling her with repugnance, the cool cologne-over-male-warmth smell of him was actually arousing her desire to move closer to its source? How was it that the solid strength of his male body against her own felt somehow right? As though it was something her flesh approved of instead of feared. It was as though she had opened a door and walked into a world that was topsy-turvy—an *Alice in Wonderland* world in which what she'd expected to feel had been replaced by the unexpected. The totally unexpected, she acknowledged as she looked with bewilderment at the way her free hand was splayed out against his chest, her skin pale next to the dark fabric of his suit.

Only seconds had passed—seconds in time but an aeon in terms of her emotions. Now, alongside the confusion of what she was feeling, she had a growing sense of urgency. A desire—no, a *need* to be free from the intimacy of his hold. And not because she feared him, but because she feared her own awareness of him.

There was an odd look in his eyes, a sort of shocked and furious disbelief, as though he couldn't fully comprehend something.

'Let me go.'

The words, echoing from her past, had a galvanising effect on her captor, banishing that look immediately and replacing it with the anger she could now see in his eyes. Anger was better—anger meant that they were enemies and on opposite sides, even though it was obvious to Lily that, whoever and whatever he was, he wasn't used to women rejecting him. His gaze was a dangerous volcano of molten gold, fixing on hers, pinning her beneath it. She could feel herself starting to tremble, weakness filling her. Tiny betraying shivers of sensation rayed out all over her body from its point of contact with his hand. Sexual awareness? Sexual desire? From her? For this man who was a stranger to her—a stranger who had already shown his bitter contempt for her? How could he have such an intense impact on her, sidetracking her away from telling him just how wrong he was about her?

Abruptly he released her, thrusting her from him, turning away from her towards the stairs and taking them two at a time, whilst she gasped for air and tried to turn the handle of the door to the studio with trembling fingers.

She was back—safe in the studio. Only Lily knew that she could never be completely safe with herself ever again. In a handful of seconds and with one automatic and instinctive male movement the protective bubble in which she had wrapped herself to defend herself against his sex had been torn from her. In his hold she had experienced an awareness of him as a man that had struck right at the core of everything she believed about herself, revealing to her a vulnerability she had promised herself she would never know. How could it have happened so quickly and so unexpectedly? So unacceptably? Like lightning striking out of nowhere? She didn't know, and she didn't want to know. She just wanted to ignore it and forget about it.

Numbly, she forced herself to go through the motions of getting back to work.

'What was all that about?' the stylist asked her curiously.

'Nothing. Just a bit of a mistake, that's all.'

A mistake it certainly had been—and the real mistake had been hers.

Her hands trembled as she adjusted the camera. Her very first memories included the feeling of being able to make herself feel safe behind a camera as she played with the equipment in her father's studio, where she had been left so often as a young child, by parents too involved in their own lives to care about hers. Her camera represented security in so many different ways. It was the magic cloak behind which she could conceal and protect herself. But not today. Not now. When she looked through her camera, instead of seeing a model posing, ready for her to photograph, all she could see was an image of the man who had just ripped the security of her self protection from her.

She closed her eyes and then opened them again. Nothing had really happened to alter her life in any way. She might feel as though she had been dragged through the eye of a storm, but that storm had gone now and she was safe.

Was she? Was she really? Or was that just what she wanted—no, needed to believe?

Her mobile beeped to warn her of an incoming text. Automatically she pressed to read it, scrolling down its length with a jerky uncoordinated touch that betrayed the effect *he* had had on her nervous system.

It was from Rick, telling her that he'd got wind of a terrific opportunity and was flying out to New York to follow up on it.

PS, he'd texted, *bkd studio in yr name. Can u pay the bill for me?*

Lily straightened her body, pushing her hair back off her face. *This* was reality—the reality of her life and her relationships. What had just happened was nothing—and meant nothing. It should be forgotten—treated as though it had never happened.

It didn't matter. It couldn't matter. For some reason a gap had opened up in the protection she had woven around herself and she had slipped into it. Slipped into it—that was all. Not fallen through it, not become lost for ever in it, spellbound by the dark magic of an unknown man's touch.

She had work to do, she reminded herself. Proper work—not stepping in to do Rick's work for him. Her real purpose in being here in Milan had nothing to do with models, or fashion, or anything that belonged to the world that had been her father's. She had her own world and her own place in it. *Her* world. Her safe, protected and protective world—and that world would never admit into it a man who could bewilder her senses to the point where he might take them prisoner.

* * *

Marco nodded to his PA, handing over to him the documents he had just signed, his mind on the rather trying and over-emotional phone call he'd just had from his sister. She was hoping, he knew, that he would take her son Pietro onto his personal staff once he had completed his university education, with a view to Pietro eventually being appointed to the board of the family business, which comprised a vast empire of various interests built up by successive generations of Lombardy nobles and merchants.

Marco's own contribution to those assets had been the acquisition of a merchant bank which had turned him into a billionaire by the time he was thirty.

Now, at thirty-three, he had turned his attention and his razor-sharp intellect away from the future to focus it instead on the past, and in particular on the artistic legacy originally created by members of his own family and those like it in financing and sponsoring artists as their protégés.

Marco had never been able to understand quite

where his older sister got her emotional intensity from. Their now dead parents had after all
been rather distant figures to them, aristocratic
and stiffly formal in the way they'd lived their
lives. The upbringing of their two children had
been left in the hands of nannies and then good
schools. Their mother hadn't been the type to
fuss over her children in any way, but especially
not physically. She had been the opposite of the
normal conception of Italian mothers—proud of
them both, Marco knew, but never one to hug
or kiss them. Not that Marco looked back on
his childhood with any sense of deprivation. His
personal space, his personal distance from other
people, was important to him.

However, he could and did understand the
concern his sister had about Pietro—even if his
keenly logical brain was not able to accept her
defence of her son's reasons for accepting money
in return for a so-called 'modelling' assignment.
Her poor son needed a more generous allowance,
she had told him, adding that it was Marco's
fault that Pietro had felt the need to take such a

risk, because Marco insisted on Pietro managing on a ridiculously small amount of money. Of course his sister has been quick to assure him that she was grateful to Marco for intervening and going to see the wicked person who had approached her precious son. After all, they both knew what could happen to young innocents who found themselves caught up in the sordid side of modelling.

Marco's gaze fell on the silver-framed photograph on his desk. Olivia, the girl in it, looked very young. The photograph had been taken just after her sixteenth birthday. Her pretty face was wreathed in a shy smile, her dark hair curling down onto her shoulders. She looked innocent and malleable, incapable of deceiving or betraying anyone. Her beauty was the beauty of a still unopened rose—there to be seen, but not yet fully mature. Olivia had never reached that maturity. Anger burned inside him—an anger that grew in intensity as out of nowhere he felt an unwanted echo of the electrical jolt of sexual awareness that had shocked through him earlier in the day, for a woman who should have been the last kind of woman on earth who could affect him like that. It had been a momentary failing, that was all, he assured himself. A consequence, no doubt, of the fact that his bed had been empty for the best part of a year, following his refusal to give in to his mistress's pleas for commitment.

He stood up and walked over to the window. He didn't particularly care for city living—or Milan. But for business reasons it made sense to keep an apartment and an office here. It was only one of several properties in his portfolio— some bought by him and some family properties inherited by him.

If he ever had to choose only one property from that portfolio it would be a magnificent castle built for one of his ancestors who himself had been a collector of the finest works of art.

Marco had been wary at first when he had been approached by Britain's Historical Preservation Trust, with a view to his helping with an exhibition being mounted in an Italian inspired English stately home that would chart the history of the

British love of Italian paintings, sculpture and architecture via various loaned artefacts, including plans, drawings and artworks. But the assurances he had received from them about the way in which the whole project would be set up and handled had persuaded him to become involved. Indeed he had become involved with it to such an extent that he had volunteered to escort the archivist the trust were sending to Italy on a preliminary tour of the Italian properties it had been decided would best fit with what the exhibition wanted to achieve.

Dr Wrightington, who had been appointed by the Historical Preservation Trust, would be touring a selection of properties selected by Marco and the trust, and Marco would be accompanying her. Her tour was to begin with a reception in Milan, after which they would visit the first properties on Marco's list—several villas on the banks of Lake Como to the North of Milan. He knew very little about Dr Wrightington other than the fact that the thesis for her doctorate had been based on the long-running historical connection between the world of Italian art and its artists, and the British patrons who had travelled to the great art studios of Rome and Florence to buy their work, returning home not just with what they had bought but also with a desire to recreate Italian architecture and design in their own homes. The tour would end at one of his own homes, the Castello di Lucchesi in Lombardy.

Marco looked at his watch, plain and without any discernible logo to proclaim its origins. Its elegance was all that was needed to declare its design status—for those rich enough to recognise it.

He had an hour before he needed to welcome Dr Wrightington to Milan at the reception he had organised for her in a castle that had originally been the home of the Sforza family—the Dukes of Milan—and what was now a public building, housing a series of art galleries. His own family had been allies of the Sforzas in earlier centuries—a relationship which had benefited both families.

CHAPTER TWO

LILY looked round her small anonymous hotel bedroom. Her bag was packed and she was ready to leave, even though it would be half an hour before the taxi would arrive.

The label on her laptop case caught her eye: Dr Lillian Wrightington. She had changed her surname just after her eighteenth birthday, to avoid association with her famous parents, taking on her maternal grandmother's maiden name.

Even now, over a year after she had been awarded her PhD, it still gave her a small thrill to see that title in front of her name.

Rick couldn't understand why she had chosen the life she had—but then how could he? His memories of their father were so different from hers.

She had had *the* dream again last night, for the

first time in ages, knowing that she was dreaming but powerless to wake herself up from it. It always followed the same course. Her father called her into the studio, telling her that she must stand in for a model who had not turned up. The thought of being photographed brought on her familiar fear. She looked for her own camera, wanting to hold it and hide behind it. Then the door to the studio opened and a man came in. His features were obscured, but Lily still knew him—and feared him. As he came towards her she tried to escape from him, calling out to her father as she did so, but he was too busy to pay her any attention. The man reached for her…

That part of the dream had been completely familiar to her. She had dreamed it a thousand times and more, after all. But then something odd had happened—something new and unfamiliar. As the horror and revulsion had risen up inside her, accompanied by anguish that her father couldn't see she needed help, the door to the studio had opened again, admitting someone else, and when she'd seen the newcomer she had been filled with relief, running to him, welcoming the feel of his fingers on her arms, knowing that despite the anger she could feel burning in him his presence would protect her and save her.

Why had she turned the man who had come to the studio Rick had hired and berated her so furiously into her rescuer? It must be because he himself felt contempt for the seedier side of modelling, and therefore at some deep level of her subconscious she had assessed him as a safe haven from those that she herself had learned so very young to fear. And was that the only reason? Lily gave a small mental shrug. What other reason could there be? What other reason did there need to be. Sometimes it was a mistake to dwell on things too deeply and to over-analyse them.

What mattered more was why she had had the dream again, after nearly three years without having it. She suspected she knew the answer to that particular question. The whole ambience of that studio had aroused too many painful unwanted memories. Memories that belonged in her past, she reminded herself determinedly. She was another person now—a person of her own creation and in her own right. Dr Lillian Wrightington, with a doctorate in the influence of Italian art and architecture on the British grand house.

Reception finally called to say her taxi was outside, and she went down to the lobby, wheeling her suitcase behind her. She was, she admitted, slightly apprehensive about meeting the Prince di Lucchesi—but only slightly. Her job as a freelancer archivist connected to the Historical Preservation Trust meant that she had attended enough fundraising events not to feel intimidated at the thought of mingling with the rich and titled. Besides in many cases, thanks to the research for her doctorate, she knew as much about the centuries of skeletons in their family cupboards as they did themselves, she reminded herself wryly.

Other academics might focus on the life of an artist responsible for certain works. She had focused instead on the patrons. Initially that had simply been so she could establish which patrons had been drawn to and bought which artist's work, but then she had found herself becoming increasingly curious about why a certain person had been drawn to a certain piece of art—or a certain artist. Human relationships were at the same time both very simple and very complicated because of the emotions that drove them—because of the mazes and minefields of problems people themselves created to control the lives of others.

She could have researched the Prince online, of course, but Lily was far more interested in men and women who inhabited the past rather than those who lived in the present. The Prince was merely someone she had to deal with in order to achieve the goal she shared with the Trust.

She had still dressed appropriately for the reception, though. First impressions mattered—especially in the world of art and money. Whilst Lily had no interest in fashion *per se*, it would have been impossible for her to have grown up the way she had without absorbing a certain sense of style. Modestly she considered that she was helped in that by her height and her slenderness. At five nine she wasn't particularly tall, but she was tall enough to carry her clothes well. Although normally when she was working she preferred to wear a tee shirt and jeans—a polo neck and jeans if it was cold, along with a fine wool long-line cardigan—for more formal public occasions such as this one she kept a wardrobe of simple good-quality outfits.

For today's reception she was wearing a caramel-coloured dress. Sleeveless, with a high slashed neckline, it skimmed the curves of her body rather than clung to them. Round her neck she was wearing the rope of pearls that had been handed down to her from her great-grandmother on her mother's side. The only other jewellery she was wearing was the Cartier watch that had been her mother's, and a pair of diamond earstuds which she had had made from the two diamonds in her mother's engagement ring.

After her mother's suicide her father had given her all her mother's jewellery. She had sold it all, apart from the watch and the engagement ring, giving the money to a charity that helped the homeless. Somehow it had seemed fitting. After all her mother's heart had become homeless, thanks to her father's affairs.

She had toned her dress with plain black accessories: good leather shoes and an equally good leather bag. Good quality, but not designer. In her case she had one of her favourite black cashmere long-line cardigans to wear later in the day for the journey from Milan to the world-famous luxurious Villa d'Este Hotel on Lake Como, where the Prince was going to escort her on a tour of some of the wonderful privately owned villas of the region at the invitation of their owners.

It was entirely due to the Prince that she was being given such a rare opportunity to see the interiors of those villas, her employer at the trust had told her, adding that it had been at the Prince's suggestion and his own expense that she was to stay at the exclusive Ville d'Este, which itself had originally been privately owned.

There was no sunshine quite like the sunshine

of late September and early October, Lily thought as the taxi negotiated the streets of Milan. Fashion week was almost over, but she still looked over when they passed the Quadrilatero d'Oro—the area that housed some of the world's most famous designer shops—before heading for the Castello Sforzesco palace.

The reception she was attending was being held within the castle, which now housed several galleries containing works of art by Italy's most famous artists. Lily was familiar with the layout of the building, having visited it whilst she had been studying for her doctorate and writing her thesis, and was a great admirer of its collections. However, after the taxi had dropped her off and she had made her way to her destination, it wasn't either the Sforza family's history or its art collections that brought her to a stunned halt in front of the double doors behind which the reception was to be held.

It was the man waiting for her there that brought a shocked, *'You!'* to her lips.

She couldn't believe it. She didn't want to believe it but it was true. He, the man from the studio who had already harangued and insulted her once, was regarding her with an expression that said just how unwelcome to him her presence was as he announced grimly, 'I don't know what you think *you* are doing here.'

Was he daring to suggest that he thought she was pursuing him? Fortunately, before she could give vent to her feelings, Lily realised that he was staring at the suitcase in front of her, where her name was written plainly on the address label.

Focusing on it, Marco read the label in growing disbelief. *Dr Lillian Wrightington.*

Removing his gaze from the label, he looked up at Lily, demanding, '*You* are Dr Wrightington?'

Lily supposed that by rights she should feel a certain sense of satisfaction at his obvious disbelief, but the reality was that it was hard for her to feel anything other than a stomach churning, knee-knocking despair. Not that she was going to let him see that. Not for one minute.

Instead she drew herself up to her full height,

tilting her chin firmly as she responded, 'Yes. And you are?'

He didn't like that, she could see. He didn't like it one tiny little bit. Anger blazed like an inquisition fire in the depths of the tawny gold eyes.

'Marco di Lucchesi,' he answered her stiffly.

The Prince? He was the Prince? Her escort for the next two weeks?'

Her leaden feeling of despair threatened to become a bubble of wild, panicked hysteria. Maybe he was just a member of the royal family. Someone sent on the Prince's behalf? Lily sent up a small prayer to fate. Please, please let that be so.

The doors behind them opened and an official came bustling out, saying when he saw Lily's case, 'Permit me to arrange for your luggage to be stored somewhere safe for you until you are ready to leave, Dr Wrightington.'

'Yes. Yes, thank you,' Lily said with a smile, before turning back to Marco to ask, dry-mouthed, 'Marco di Lucchesi? Prince di Lucchesi?'

'I do not use the title.' His curt response blew away her fragile hopes like a tornado attacking soap bubbles. 'If you are ready I will escort you inside and make some introductions for you. Several of the families whose homes you will be seeing are represented amongst those attending the reception.'

Lily inclined her head.

'The Historical Preservation Trust supplied me with a copy of the guest list.'

'Some of the family trees are rather complex. It is not always easy to know who owns what.'

Not for the ordinary English tourist, perhaps, but Italian genealogy where it related to grand houses and villas were her field of expertise. It was a sign of how much seeing him had shaken her that she did not feel like pointing that out to him, Lily acknowledged. Nevertheless she knew that it was war between them, with gauntlets thrown down and challenges made. Language could be every bit as filled with subtle textures that held concealed messages as art.

Her suitcase had been wheeled away. Marco was standing to one side of her, and the doors— her escape route—were directly in front of her. Refusing to look at him, Lily headed determinedly for them.

She almost made it—would have made it, in fact, if at the last minute he hadn't beaten her to the doors, with Machiavellian timing and a male stride that easily outpaced her high-heeled gait. He barred her escape by the simple expedient of placing his arm across the closed doors.

There was nowhere for her to go—nothing for her to do other than either stand where she was, a safe couple of feet away from him, or walk into him.

Walk into him? In a series of images inside her head she could see the physical contact there had already been between them. She could feel again her own inexplicable reaction to it. The ante-room was empty, the air in it cool, but she could feel perspiration breaking out along her hair-line. Why had this had to happen? Why had he had to come into her life?

Wasn't there an even more important question she should be asking herself? her inner critic taunted her. Shouldn't she really be asking why he disturbed her so much? Why his mere presence was enough to cause a scarily powerful undertow of emotions and sensations within her?

He'd touched her first. And, like her, he had recoiled at that first contact as though he had suffered the same shock of sensation and awareness that had electrified her. That should surely have put them on a level battleground. But somehow it had not. Somehow he remained in possession of the higher ground.

It didn't matter what he had or had not experienced, Lily told herself protectively. What mattered was what had always mattered to her, and that was maintaining her own security— emotionally, mentally and physically.

Marco frowned. What was that scent she was wearing? It was so delicate and alluring that it made him want to move closer to her to catch its true essence. Which no doubt was exactly why she was wearing it so sparingly, he thought cynically, reminding himself that he had far more substantial and important questions he wanted answers to than the name of her scent.

'Does the trust know about the kind of work you do in your spare time?'

He was threatening her, or at least attempting to threaten her, Lily recognized. Even if he had not put that threat into exact words. Anger and fear burned a caustic path over her emotional nerve-endings. He was wrong about her. He was misjudging her. He probably thought he was far too important for her to risk offending him by standing up to him. She had a right to defend herself, though, and that was exactly what she was going to do—as little as she liked being put in a position where she had to explain herself to him.

'I wasn't working—as such. I was simply doing a favour for…for a friend, and standing in for them at the last minute.' It was the truth, after all.

Marco felt his anger against her grow and burn even more hotly. She was playing with words, using those that suited her and discarding those that did not. Just as she played with the vulnerable young lives of silly young fools like his nephew. 'So the trust doesn't know?'

'There is nothing for them *to* know. I did a favour for…for someone, and—'

'A favour? Is that what you call it? I have a very different name for what you were doing.'

How could this woman, this Dr Lillian Wrightington, be the same woman he had caught trying to bribe his nephew into modelling for her?

It seemed impossible…but it wasn't. Quite plainly Dr Wrightington was a woman who lived two very separate lives. What could possibly motivate a woman highly qualified and presumably able to command a respectable salary to involve herself in such sleaze? The anger and pain he had felt over Olivia's death surged through him. He could taste it in his mouth, feel it burning his emotions.

They had been childhood friends, expected by their families to marry one day. Theirs would have been a platonic union, a business arrangement, and Olivia had assured him that she wanted the same thing, too. Only she'd been leading a secret life, duped into chasing fame as a model, and it cut deep to think that the girl he'd thought he knew had been deceiving him all that time.

Olivia had never found that fame. Drugs and ultimately prostitution had dragged her into the gutter and from there to her death, and her journey there had been facilitated by a woman like the one standing in front of him now. A woman who bought beautiful young flesh for those with a taste for it, and who deceived those who possessed that beautiful young flesh with promises of fame and fortune.

He had trusted both Olivia herself and that woman, but they had both lied to him about their intentions. That knowledge had left a raw wound within him that his pride could not allow to heal. They'd given him their word, their promise, they'd taken his trust and destroyed it. He'd have to be a complete fool—a weak, easily manipulated fool—to trust another woman now. His cynicism burned inside him like vitriol.

'Why do you do it?' he asked grimly.

Lily could feel the icy-cold blast of his contempt like a burn against her skin. It made her want to shrink into herself in anguished pain. What had she ever done to warrant his harshness towards her? Nothing. And yet the knowledge that he felt contempt for her pierced her. What was it about him that made her own emotions react so deeply to him? As though somehow she was hyper-sensitive to him—as though some kind of magnetic link existed between them, enclosing her and making her acutely vulnerable to the force-field of his personality, no matter how hard she struggled to resist the effect he was having on her.

'Why do I do what?'

'Don't pretend not to understand me. You know perfectly well what I mean—that seedy studio, the manner in which you approached my nephew.'

His words brought a guilty flush of colour to
her skin, even though she had nothing to feel
guilty about.

'I've already told you I was simply doing someone else a favour.'

Far from placating him, her explanation served
only to add to his biting contempt.

'I can imagine the kind of *favour* you were
attempting to do,' he told her brutally, the fury
inside him spilling over. 'Tell me something,' he
demanded. 'Does what you're doing never worry
you? Do you ever give any thought to the damage
and destruction you and your kind cause?'

Lily's heart had started to thump heavily and
uncomfortably. She was beginning to feel panicked by his attack. He was advancing into private territory within her that was filled with
thinly healed sores. It was incredibly ironic that
he should make the assumptions about her that
he had. Incredibly ironic and almost unbearable.
Only her keenly honed instinct to protect herself
stopped her from protesting and from justify-
ing her involvement. Instead, as calmly as she

could, she said unsteadily, 'As I've already told you—not that I need to explain or excuse my actions to *you*—I was asked by my…by someone to take over a photographic shoot for a clothes catalogue. Nothing more than that.'

'So what about the young man who was approached in a student bar and offered the opportunity of doing some modelling work in this shoot? Didn't that worry you? Didn't you question your…*friend* about why he had found a model in such a way? There are, after all, model agencies who I am sure have books filled with the names of young men who already know at least some of the pitfalls of the business in which they are involved.'

Lily could feel the sting of his words against her emotions, lacerating and flaying them as effectively as though he had laid a whip to her flesh. The only difference was that the wounds he was inflicting on her she could and must keep hidden from him. In the life she had so carefully created for herself there was no place for the girl she had once been and there never would be.

She had cut herself off from her past to protect herself from her own ghosts. She would never look back at them.

Because she was still afraid of them?

Why was this happening to her? She had been so happy, so safe, had felt a real pride in herself and what she had achieved, and now because of one man—this man—who was determined to misjudge her, everything she had was in jeopardy. The desire to give in to her emotions had never been stronger, but Lily knew that she had to overcome that desire. Calmness, logic and knowing the truth must be her weapons in this fight, and she must wield them well if she was to protect herself.

Lily took a deep breath,

'Clothing catalogues don't exactly pay top dollar. My…the person I was helping wanted to keep his costs down. That was why he approached your nephew. No other reason.'

'Do you really expect me to believe that? It's illogical. After all, in addition to paying my nephew your friend also suggested he accompany him to a post-shoot party with some of fashion's big names.'

This was too much. Lily could feel her defences crumbling. She had really had enough. She wasn't at all happy about being put in the position of having to defend her half-brother's behaviour, but neither did she think Marco di Lucchesi's behaviour towards her was in any way acceptable.

He had virtually accused her of acting on behalf of a pervert bent on corrupting the innocence of his nephew. Rick had his faults, but he would only have been trying to impress his potential models—nothing more.

'You're mistaken about Rick,' she insisted fiercely, 'and about me.' When he didn't respond she added impulsively, 'If you want the truth, I feel exactly the same way about the sleazy side of modelling as you do.'

Wasn't that more or less exactly what the owner of the model agency Olivia had worked for had told him when he had gone to her for help in his quest to bring Olivia safely home? When Olivia herself had refused to listen to him? Hadn't the woman told him that she shared his opinion of Olivia's vulnerability and that he could trust her to protect and keep her safe? Eighteen-year-old Marco had foolishly believed her, but she had been lying, and so too was the woman confronting him now. Past experience and the facts told him that.

Why, then, when it should have been the simplest of matters to continue to denounce her, without any compunction and without any kind of emotional reaction himself, was he now discovering that it wasn't? What was stopping him? For some inexplicable reason, and completely illogically, he was actually experiencing an unwanted but undeniable emotional reaction to her deceit. Why? Why should he care that she was a liar who couldn't be trusted? He didn't, Marco assured himself, and told her curtly, 'What you're saying does not add up, therefore it cannot possibly be true.'

Lily stared at him in stunned disbelief. Everything about his body language and the look on his face told her that nothing she could say would change his mind. He was calling her a liar, and he was making it plain that he wasn't going to change his mind—no matter what she tried to say. It was as though he wanted to dislike and distrust her. Very well, she would defend herself by using the same 'logic' on him that he had used against her.

'No one forced your nephew to accept the photo shoot, the money, or the party invitation,' she pointed out, somehow managing to adopt a cool, clear, emotionless voice. 'Instead of harassing me you might do better using your bullying questioning tactics on him. After all, a young man so well connected and coming from such a wealthy family shouldn't need to accept work that pays so little—unless, of course, he had other reasons for accepting it.'

She had hit a nerve now, Lily recognised. He might not have betrayed it in any visible way, but she knew as surely as if the reaction had been hers that inwardly he had recoiled from her challenge.

'What reasons?

His voice was harsh, almost raw with an emotion that was more than anger—as though something had been dredged up from deep within him against his will. Lily could feel herself weakening. Only he was not a man for whom she should feel compassion, she warned herself. In his way he was every bit as dangerous as those he was castigating, if not more so.

Taking a deep breath, she challenged him silkily. 'An uncle who keeps him on too short a rope, perhaps?'

He didn't like it. He didn't like it one little bit. And yet to her surprise, instead of retreating into an angry and arrogant princely silence, no doubt meant to indicate to her that he did not have to explain himself or his actions to someone as plebeian as she, he told her, 'Pietro is a young man with a tendency to behave impulsively and the belief that he is immortal. Traits which in my opinion are the result of a little too much maternal indulgence. If I believe he should be able to manage within his not ungenerous allowance then I do so in the knowledge that one day he will be responsible for managing a far greater sum of money. You may think that to be keeping him on a short rope. I consider it to be encouraging him to respect the benefits of living within his means.'

'Perhaps that is something you should be telling him, not me?' Lily suggested. 'I accept that your nephew is important to you, but what is important to me right now is doing what the Trust sent me here to do.' She looked pointedly at the closed doors he had barred.

'And you can be trusted to carry out that duty, can you? Without disappearing to undertake some very different work on the side for a "friend"?'

'You have neither the right nor any reason to question my commitment to my work.'

'On the contrary, I have both the right—since I am responsible for persuading people to admit you into their homes—and the reason you have already supplied to me.'

'We are keeping people waiting,' Lily reminded

him, anxious to bring their conversation to a close and to escape from him. She looked at the door, but he was standing closer to it than she was and he was watching her.

CHAPTER THREE

THE way Marco was looking at her was making Lily's heart thump raggedly with tension. If only someone would come and interrupt them, bring her torment to an end. But no one did, and she was left with no alternative other than to listen to him.

'I don't accept for one minute that the motives of you or your friend were as altruistic as you would have me believe,' he told her.

'I'm telling you the truth. If you can't accept that then that's your problem.'

'No,' he told her harshly. 'You are *not* telling me the truth.'

His presence encircled her now. She could neither step forward nor back. He had bent his head to speak quietly into her ear, and now a thousand delicate nerve-endings were being tortured by the warmth of his breath. She felt hot and dizzy, with a torrent of sensations cascading through her caused by the fact that he had breached the polite barrier of personal space that should have existed between them.

She had to say something. She had to stand her ground. But she could hardly breathe, never mind that her flesh was almost screaming out a feral cry of panicked fear. She tried to step past him, but he moved even more swiftly, causing her to cannon into him.

Her small gasp grazed the bare skin of Marco's neck, causing an explosion of sensual pleasure to bomb his nerve-endings and race from them along his veins like liquid fire. His response to it was so instinctive and automatic that he was reaching for her before his brain knew what was happening. Frantically it searched for an explanation for what he was feeling. How could he, a man who could quite easily remain impervious to the most blatant of erotic sensual persuasion from the women who had shared his bed, have succumbed so easily to the mere touch of her breath against his skin? What was it about this woman that ripped aside his self-control and induced in him such a primitive male response?

Of course he would release her; there was, after all no purpose in him holding her. No purpose and certainly no desire, he assured himself—and he would have released her too, if she hadn't started to struggle against him, igniting a feeling inside him that came like a thunderbolt out of nowhere to challenge his male pride.

'No!' Panic had filled Lily at the way her body was reacting to the proximity of his body, as though it actually *wanted* that proximity, and she desperately needed to bring it to an end before he realised the effect he was having on her. But now, as she saw the look in his eyes, Lily realised that he had misinterpreted her anxiety as defiance—and she could see too that he intended to punish her for it.

That punishment was swift and shocking. His mouth taking hers in a kiss of blistering male revenge that seared her senses. It had been years since she had last been kissed—and never, ever like this. Never, ever in a way that imprinted everything about the male lips possessing hers on her senses and her psyche, from the texture of his skin to its taste. In a thousand rapid-fire shutter actions his maleness was being matched by her femaleness. Why? What was happening to her?

Lily lifted her free hand in protest, her eyes opening and widening when her fingertips grazed the flesh of his face. She could feel the contrast between the skin of his jaw where he'd shaved and the skin above it. The photographer in her, the artist, wanted to explore the lines of his face, so dramatically perfect. *She* wanted to. Her lips softened and parted. So that she could protest. It had to be for that. It couldn't be for anything else. And that small mewing sound locked in the back of her throat? That was a complaint, she assured herself.

His own eyes were open now, his gaze a dangerous volcano of molten gold fixing on hers. She could feel herself starting to tremble, weakness filling her, so that she was forced to lean into him. Into him and onto him.

There was a moment in space and time during which it seemed to Lily that their bodies moved together of their own volition—and then abruptly he was pushing her away from him.

What was happening to him? He never normally allowed emotion to control his behaviour. Never.

Someone was trying to open the door from the other side. Without looking at one another, never mind speaking to one another, they both stepped back from it. As swiftly and determinedly as he intended to step back from what he had felt holding her in his arms, her lips clinging to his, Marco told himself, acknowledging grimly as he did so that he had been right to have doubts about the wisdom of this project. He should have trusted his instincts and refused to get involved. The trouble was when he had had those doubts it had never for one minute crossed his mind just *why* he had been right to have them. It had been the ability of a foreign organisation in a foreign country to do justice to the history of Italy in general and his own family in particular that had made him feel wary about the project.

Now, though, he was having to deal with a far more immediate and personal cause for concern. And that was…

He snatched a brief, hard glance at Lily. On the face of it there was no immediately discernible reason why his flesh should be so aware of hers, or so responsive to it. No discernible reason why his senses should so attuned to her presence, her scent, the shadow cast by her body, the sound of her breathing, the lift of her breasts as she did so. Grinding his teeth against the way his thoughts were running free, he battled to bring them back in order, straining the muscles of his self-control just as controlling runaway horses and chariot would have strained the muscles of an experienced Roman gladiator.

She was attractive enough—quietly and discreetly beautiful, even. In a way that blended perfectly with her current persona whilst being completely at odds with the persona she had revealed in the studio—her real persona, he was sure. And was that the persona to which he was attracted? Like a schoolboy aroused by the thought of the pseudo-wantonness of a naked centrefold model? Was there deep within him a hitherto unknown part that was attracted to and aroused by such a woman? The thought revolted him, and it told him all he wanted to know about his real feelings. A part of him would have preferred that to be the truth rather than having to admit the actual truth—which was that his body was every bit as responsive to her in her present role as Dr Lillian Wrightington as it had been to the streetwise, jean-clad, predatory woman.

So physically he had responded to her? What did that mean? Nothing. Nothing at all. He would not allow it to mean anything.

Holding the door open for her, Marco told Lily in a curt voice, 'I shall be watching you, Dr Wrightington, and if I suspect for any reason that your presence here is compromising the success of this project I shall have no hesitation in getting in touch with the trust and requesting them to replace you with someone else.'

'You can't do that,' Lily protested. Her mouth had gone dry and her heart was thumping unevenly. This project meant so much to her. There'd even been talk of it being covered for a very well thought of TV arts programme. More than the career benefits that kind of exposure would bring her, though, Lily wanted to share with a wider audience the huge impact Italian art brought back to Britain had had on so many aspects of British life—from architecture to literature, from gardening to fashion, and so much more. To be dismissed from this project was the last thing she wanted.

Marco was a powerful man, and one who was already prejudiced against her. What was that sharp stab of anguish all about? She didn't care what he thought about her. He could misjudge her as much as he wished. In fact she was glad that he had. Was she? Was she really?

Marco was still holding the door open. The buzz of conversation from the people gathered inside the room receded like an ebbing tide, until there was nothing left apart from a rustling silence as everyone looked towards them.

Whilst she felt uncomfortable, her companion seemed completely composed and in control, announcing, 'Please accept my apologies for the fact that we are a little late. The blame is entirely mine.'

And he would be forgiven for it, Lily could tell. The smiles being directed towards him were both admiring and respectful. No one, it seemed, wished to question or query the Prince di Lucchesi.

'I know you are all impatient to talk with our guest of honour, Dr Wrightington, so I think I shall dispense with a lengthy speech and just say instead that her scholarship in the subject of the art collected by our predecessors and the architecture of our homes should speak for itself.'

Had anyone other than her noticed that questioning 'should'? Lily wondered, thankful of the poise she had learned from observing her mother—before heartache and prescription pills had destroyed her. It was surprisingly easy to stand tall with a smile pinned to your face once you'd learned the trick of hiding the reality of what you were feeling within yourself.

Easy, too, to make small talk as she circled the floor at Marco's side whilst he introduced her to people with names that were woven into the very fabric of this part of Italy's.

'Your Grace.' Lily responded to Marco's introduction to an elderly duchess with a formidably upright bearing. 'I can't thank you enough for allowing me to see your villa and your art collection. There is a wonderful sketch in the archives at Castle Howard of one of your ancestors, drawn—'

'By Leonardo. Yes, I have heard of it. Although sadly I have never seen it.'

Lily smiled at her. 'I was given permission to photograph it so that I could show it to you.'

She was impressive, Marco acknowledged reluctantly. Not just in her knowledge of her subject but also in her manner—but how much of her was learned and how much the real woman? Not very much, he decided.

'It will be interesting to compare it with the painting of my husband's ancestor by Leonardo,' the Duchess told Lily with a smile.

Normally Lily enjoyed this kind of occasion— the opportunity to talk with people who shared her interests and her love of Italian art—but today for some reason, after less than a couple of hours of mingling with the other guests, she developed the beginnings of a very painful pounding stress headache that made her feel slightly sick.

For *some* reason? She was supposed to be an intelligent woman. The reason for her tension was standing less than two yards away from her, and right now she could feel his gaze burning into her back. So the man running the project here in Italy was hostile to her and contemptuous of her—so what? She more than most people was adept at cocooning herself in her own private emotional and mental space and not allowing others to penetrate that space. Adept at it? She was an expert in it, Lily acknowledged wryly. In fact if there was a degree to be had in it she would have graduated first class with honours.

'It will soon be time for us to leave.'

The sound of Marco's voice from directly behind her had Lily almost choking on the sip of wine she had just taken. Not because she hadn't heard him move—she had. She was acutely aware of every single move he made. What she hadn't been prepared for was the warmth of his breath on the nape of her neck, where it was revealed by the soft knot of her drawn back hair. Was it just because he had caught her off-guard that she had felt the shower of tiny darts that had now brought her skin out in goosebumps? Goosebumps of delicious sensual pleasure?

Lily knew that it wasn't. She wasn't even going to begin question how it was that a person who had turned her back on the delights of sexual pleasure should immediately be able to recognise and understand that the degree of sensuality she had just experienced spoke of a vulnerability to the man who had caused it that went far beyond the norm of casual sexual attraction. Some questions were better not asked—especially by someone like her—when they involved someone like Marco.

When a man standing in a group to her right moved, accidentally nudging her arm and causing some of her wine to spill from her glass onto her bare skin, Lily was relieved—grateful, in fact, for the small incident. It distracted her attention and Marco's far too perceptive and sharp gaze from her earlier involuntary shudder of delight.

'I'm so sorry,' the man apologised, telling a passing waiter, 'We need a dry cloth, please.'

'There's no need...' Lily began to say, but the words became locked in her throat as out of nowhere, or so it seemed, Marco himself produced a white cloth, which he placed on her damp arm. He ignored her panicky, 'I can do it myself,' just as he ignored her attempt to move away from him. Somehow he had taken possession of both her nearly empty glass, which he had placed on the tray of a hovering waiter, and her damp arm, his hand and his fingers lean and tanned against the white starched fabric of the cloth. He had good hands, Lily acknowledged. Strong artist's hands. Hands with a powerful male grip that could crush a woman's resistance to their hold should he feel it necessary.

A new quiver forked through her. Not on her flesh this time, but deep within it—a swift, tightening, convulsive sensation that gripped and then relaxed, leaving a far too intimate pulse beating in its place.

Lily was perfectly familiar with the outward signs of sexual arousal. After all she had seen models mimicking them in one form or another for as long as she could remember. Bitterly she recalled how when her father had finished working she would be pushed into the small boxroom off his studio whilst he 'played'. Her father had been of that order of photographers in a certain era who had believed that having sex with models was one of the perks of the job. No, she was no stranger to the signs and sounds of physical arousal, both real and faked, male and female, but when it came to being familiar with her own sexual arousal… That was haunted, poisoned territory that had long ago become an empty wasteland and she didn't go there. She didn't want to go there.

Marco was releasing her.

'It's time for us to go,' he told her. 'The traffic to the airport will be heavy at this time of the day.'

'The airport? We're flying to Lake Como?'

She'd assumed that they'd be driving there.

'By helicopter. It's much the easier way to get there,' Marco informed her, clapping his hands for silence so that he could announce their departure.

'I was already looking forward to introducing you to Villa Ambrosia,' the Duchess told Lily, coming over to say goodbye to her and holding both Lily's hands in her own as she did so, in a gesture of genuine liking and approval. 'But now that I have met you I am looking forward to it even more. She is a delightful girl, Marco,' she added, turning to him. 'Look after her well, won't you?'

Of course Lily didn't dare look at Marco once the Duchess had left them and they were on their own. The Duchess's comment about his looking after her wouldn't have gone down at all well, she suspected.

The museum official who had taken her case and insisted on wheeling it for her escorted them to their waiting car. It would be very easy to get used to such a pampered way of life, Lily thought, remembering ruefully how often she had ended up with an aching back from a bulging bag holding her laptop, her camera, and assorted other necessary paraphernalia for her work.

The traffic was heavy, but the insulated interior of the luxurious saloon car protected them from the fume-clogged air outside. A glass screen separated them from the driver, and the combination of that and the soft leather of their seats made Lily feel that they were isolated together in a space that was far too intimate.

Not that there was any intimacy between the two of them. Marco had produced his cell phone the minute the chauffeur had closed the door of the car, his brief, 'Please excuse me,' immediately distancing him from her. Because he *wanted* to be distanced from her? Of course he did. He despised her. Lily knew that was true, but she also knew that—like her—he had felt the startling electric connection that had burned into life between them the first time he had touched her. A connection that neither of them wanted.

Now Marco was putting his phone down and turning towards her.

'Just before we left the reception the Duchess asked me if there was any chance that we might be able to spend a couple of nights at her villa as her guests. You obviously made a very big impression on her.'

The stiff hostility in his voice told Lily how little he liked telling her that.

'I've just been checking through our schedule.

It would be possible for us to extend the tour to include a short stay with her if you wish to do so.'

So he hadn't been distancing himself from her. He had actually been working on her behalf, or rather on behalf of their shared project, Lily was forced to admit reluctantly. She didn't want to have to feel guilty about misjudging him, but it seemed that she was going to have to admit that she had. Just as he had misjudged her—although she suspected she would never be able to convince him of that. Not after everything that had happened between them. Not that she was going to even attempt to change his mind about her. Why should she want to?

Still, she couldn't help but wonder what had caused such a deep-rooted loathing of what he believed she represented. Whatever it was, she couldn't imagine him ever telling her about it. Everything about him said that he simply wasn't the kind of man who confided in other people. He was too remote for that, too proud, Lily thought tiredly as she forced herself to respond with professional politeness.

'It's very generous of her to make such a kind offer. I'd love to have the opportunity to spend more time studying both the villa and her art collection.'

'Very well, then. I'll e-mail an acceptance of her invitation to her personal assistant.'

The chauffeur swung the car out of the static traffic and into a space he had spotted in the adjacent lane. Automatically Lily put her hand down to stop herself from sliding along the leather seat, but to her embarrassment felt only the hard, unyielding surface of Marco's thigh.

Scarlet-faced with mortification, she snatched her hand away. Was it her imagination or were her fingertips tingling with awareness of the flesh they had accidentally touched? It was certainly her imagination that was providing her with unwanted and dangerous images of charcoal sketches of a taut male thigh. Marco's thigh.

'We'll be at the airport in a few minutes.'

The calmly delivered information should have been enough to block out such images but somehow it wasn't. Lily kept her face turned towards the car window as they approached the airport. She didn't dare risk looking directly at Marco. Not that he could see what had been going on inside her head, of course. Thank goodness.

From his own corner of the comfortable limousine Marco cursed under his breath at the effect Lily's brief touch on his thigh had had on him. Because he hadn't been expecting it, that was all. There was nothing special about her touch that could have caused that almost violent surge of unstoppable desire from stabbing up his thigh and into his groin. He had been so involved in his business affairs that he hadn't realised until now just how long he had been celibate. Too long. That was what had made him vulnerable to her. Nothing else. His intellect and his emotions were appalled by the very idea that he could find her physically desirable, given what he knew about her. She was a woman whose way of life he had very good reason to abhor—a woman he had already discovered to be involved in the same kind of world that had destroyed Olivia.

Olivia.

Lured away by promises of the fame her beauty could bring her as a top model, Olivia had been seduced by the thought of excitement and adventure far from the safety and security of her sheltered life with her parents.

It had taken him several weeks to discover that she had moved to London. He had pleaded with her to come home but she'd refused. She had told him that she had been taken on by a modelling agency and had been sharing a flat with other young models.

He had gone to see the owner of the model agency and appealed to her for help. She had seemed so sympathetic and understanding, so concerned for Olivia, that he had made the mistake of believing her when she had assured him that he had her personal guarantee that Olivia would be safe in her care, and that she would quickly tire of her new life and decide to return home.

At eighteen, he had been a gullible fool. How that knowledge still burned like acid within him.

He'd had no idea that the woman was little more than a procuress, and that far from protecting the girls in her charge she was selling them into a life of drugs and prostitution. That life had led ultimately to Olivia dying from an overdose, alone in a New York hotel room.

He had buried his shame, his gullibility, his guilt deep within himself, making a vow to himself that his days of trusting others were over and that in future he would rely on logic and not emotion to direct the course of his life.

Until now—until Dr Lillian Wrightington, with her lies and her connection with all that he loathed—he had had no difficulty whatsoever in keeping that vow. But now, in the short time that he had known her, she had not only undermined that resolution she had also found a fault line in his defences that was causing all his long-buried vulnerabilities to rise like ghosts to mock and taunt him.

What went on inside the head of a woman like her to enable her to live a double life without guilt, to tell her lies with such passionate conviction?

Against his will Marco found that his gaze was drawn to Lily's averted profile, as though by studying it he might somehow find the answer. Very quickly he realised his mistake. His brain might only seek to study and analyse the facts, but his body was reacting to her on a very different and very dangerous level indeed. And was that reaction outside his control? Of course not, he denied. But he still had to move discreetly in his seat, in order to ease the pressure of his unwanted arousal. And whilst he did so his gaze insisted on remaining fixed on her.

Why? He tried to look away, but a few small wisps had escaped from the soft knot of her hair, catching his attention and sending his senses down a dangerous course at such high speed that to stop them was impossible.

She was looking downwards, that he could see the dark fan of her lashes and the shadows they threw across her face. The downbent angle of her neck revealed the vulnerability of its exposed nape. She had a small beauty spot just to one side of the top bone of her spine, just where a lover would be unable to resist the temptation to kiss it and then work his way along her slender throat to her ear, and then back down again to her collarbone. Her skin would smell and taste of the scent that surrounded her, which reminded him vaguely of roses and lavender. Her bare arms were slender and toned, and lightly tanned. Her wristwatch was slightly loose on her wrist. Her dress might not cling to her body, but he had watched her earlier at the reception as she mingled with the other guests. She must know that the way it subtly hinted at the swell of her breasts and the curves of her waist and hips was far, far more sensually alluring than something tight would have been.

Marco tried to control his wayward thoughts, but doing so was like trying to swim a river at full tide—every effort he made to reach the safety of logic only resulted in him being swept further into the dangerous current of his senses.

The very fact that her dress obscured rather

than revealed her body aroused the hunter him, made him want to confirm for himself that the secrets of her body were every bit as pleasurable to his gaze and his touch as he suspected. She was temptation in a dozen different ways. *Deliberate* temptation, Marco warned himself, remembering the manner in which she walked, her posture upright, her head held proudly on the slender stem of her neck, whilst at the same time being so careful not to sway her hips, not to attract attention to her femininity. It only served to build a man's appetite to know more of her. The ache in his body intensified. He needed to think of something else, of someone else, but somehow he couldn't. He couldn't think of anything other than her.

And it wasn't just his own sex she had won over at the reception. The women there had liked her as well. She had seen the approving looks they had given her, and the way in which even the most regal of them had unbent whilst talking with her. The Duchess's invitation was proof of that.

No, he couldn't deny that she was well versed in her subject, and also able to share her own obvious love for it with others, so that they too became enthused.

If he hadn't known about her other life, her other self, Marco suspected that he too might have become an admirer of her familiarity with her subject. And an admirer of her too?

No!

He had never believed in mixing work with pleasure, Marco reminded himself. It always led to complications and problems. But his role within this project was a voluntary one, taken on because of his own pleasure and pride in his own heritage.

No! His answer to his own question was still the same.

He did not want her. He could not want her. But neither could he deny the fact that his body found something physically compelling about her. It was an awkward reality he could well have done without.

Marco forced his thoughts back into the channels where they belonged. They had reached the airport, and the driver was turning off for the private part of the airfield, where expensive-looking executive jets awaited their passengers and owners. He checked his watch. They were running slightly late, but he had e-mailed ahead to warn the helicopter pilot to alter their departure slot. He could see the chopper up ahead of them on the runway, the pilot already on board. The driver brought the limousine to a smooth halt a mere handful of yards away from the helicopter and then got out to open the rear passenger door for Lily, whilst one of the waiting attendants removed their cases from the boot.

After a few words with the waiting concierge whilst she stood to one side, Marco indicated that she should board the helicopter. When she hesitated, Marco frowned. He could see her hand was gripping the handrail to the steps, her bones showing through her delicate skin. Her face had lost some of its colour, and she looked like someone screwing up every last bit of her courage to make herself do something that terrified her.

Her fear had somehow stripped her features of their maturity, so that instead of a grown woman Marco felt he was looking at a terrified child. A terrified child who was staring blindly into space as though locked away—trapped—in a world of dreadful fear.

Reluctantly, trying to check himself but unable to do so, and against all the urgings of his brain, as though some deep-rooted recognition was overriding his logic, he felt the most extraordinary and unexpected feeling of concern and compassion for that child fill him.

'You don't like flying?' he guessed. 'There is nothing to worry about if you haven't flown in a helicopter before. Come...' Why was he behaving like this? Treating her as though... Before he could stop himself, Marco was holding out his hand to her.

Without thinking Lily placed her own hand within Marco's. She felt slightly sick and light-headed, and the warmth of his hand wrapping round her own was a reassuring comfort she could feel at a distance, as though she was standing outside herself, observing her own reactions.

It was crazy to let the thought of flying in a helicopter affect her like this just because once before someone had taken her hand, urged her up the steps to a similar machine. Once before a man had smiled at her and reassured her that she would be perfectly safe—before his smile had disappeared in an explosion of anger and a fierce tug on her arm that had dragged her up into the dark interior of a helicopter.

The hand Marco was holding started to tremble, the small vibrations seizing her arm and then her whole body. Perspiration broke out on her skin, bathing her in an uncomfortable wash of anxious heat.

People were waiting…watching… She must get a grip.

'There is nothing to be afraid of,' Marco repeated. 'But if you prefer—if it makes you feel more comfortable—we can travel by road.'

His voice was calm, his grip on her hand loosening slightly as he stroked his thumb over her frantically racing pulse.

Lily turned her head and looked at him. His eyes were topaz-gold, not pale blue, and nor were they filled with a look of greedy desire that filled her with fear and revulsion. His stance was still and patient, his manner towards her soothingly reassuring, as though…as though he understood. She took a deep breath.

'No. It's all right. I'll be all right now.'

A small tug of her hand freed it from his grip, and an equally small nod of his head gave her the courage to make her way up the steps, to be helped into the machine by the uniformed co-pilot who introduced himself to her and then escorted her to her seat, showing her how to fasten herself properly into it before telling her cheerfully. 'We'll have you up at Lake Como and Villa d'Este in no time at all.'

When the man then fastened himself into the seat next to her, Lily was surprised—until he explained with another smile, 'The boss will be taking the co-pilot's seat up-front. He's a fully qualified pilot, although on this trip he'll just be playing a watching role.'

Somehow she wasn't surprised that Marco was a pilot. He had all the necessary skills, and she could easily imagine him remaining calm and focused, no matter what kind of crisis he was obliged to face.

The last time she had flown in a helicopter she had been fourteen years old. Lily's stomach muscles clenched. It was memories of that trip that had sparked off her reaction to boarding this machine now, but somehow or other Marco had found a way to break through her fear and bring her back to the present. Lily suspected that he would be anything but pleased to know that her senses had decided to recognise him as their protector and saviour. She found it hard to understand herself, given his hostility towards her.

When the shape of his body briefly obscured the light coming in through the glass nose of the machine Lily's heart jerked as though someone had deliberately pulled on its strings. She recognised that seeing him there now, on board the helicopter, was somehow extraordinarily comforting. How could that be when there was such conflict between them? Lily didn't know. She only knew that something deep inside her followed its own path and saw something in him that represented a safe haven.

A safe haven. For so many years of her life she had longed for that—for a presence, a person, who would take her side and protect her. But she had learned then that for her there was no such presence or person, and that she would have to provide her own protection and places of safety.

Now, cruelly, there was every bit as much danger for her in listening to that insistent instinct that was filling her subconscious with powerful images of safety and protection in the form of Marco di Lucchesi. That was because another instinct, every bit as powerful and demanding, was filling her senses and her body with a very different kind of awareness—the awareness of Marco as a man with the power to arouse her sexuality.

Safety and danger forged together in a complete and exact reversal of what she normally thought of as safety and danger.

Until now, until Marco, for her safety had been her own determined separation of herself from her sexuality, her sacrifice of it in order to protect herself from the danger of repeating the errors of her parents' hedonistic lifestyles. Until now and Marco *she* had been the one who was in charge of her security. Now without her being able to do a thing about it, control of her sexuality and her security had transferred itself from her into the hold of a man who despised and disliked her. How could that be? Lily didn't know. What she did know, though, was that she was not likely to be in any danger from her growing sensual and sexual responsiveness to Marco—at least not from him. She might not have known him for very long, but she knew instinctively that he would not allow himself to give in to any desire he felt for a woman he did not like.

She looked out of the window and down at the land beneath them. It was too dark for her to see anything other than the lights from the homes and roads below them.

'Soon be there now.' The co-pilot's voice was kind, but it lacked Marco's note of authority and safety which struck such a strong deep chord inside her. Just being held by him, even when he was angry with her, made her feel… Lily could feel her face beginning to burn as she felt a sudden fierce ache of pure female sexual desire stab through her. She wanted Marco. Oh, the irony of that! An irony that only she would ever know and understand.

They were coming in to land. Lily had imposed a steel band of rejection over what she was feeling, but it melted like snow in the full glare of a midsummer sun when Marco turned round to look at her. If only things were different. If only they were coming here as lovers. If only…

How could such preposterously foolish thoughts have managed to put down roots inside her emotions? Lily didn't know. She was just thankful that Marco di Lucchesi couldn't see them. Very thankful indeed.

CHAPTER FOUR

THEIR flight had been smooth and uneventful—and, given both that and the nature of his perfectly understandable feelings of distrust and contempt for Lily Wrightington, Marco was at a loss to explain to himself just why he found it necessary to hang back now that they could disembark from the helicopter, just so that he could keep a watch over her. Just as hard to explain was the concern he had felt for her during the short flight—to the point where he had had to actively restrain himself from turning round in his seat to check that she was all right.

She *wasn't* a vulnerable child, no matter what emotive mental images his head had produced to that effect. She was a fully grown woman. A deceitful, amoral, not-to-be trusted woman, who preyed on the vulnerabilities of others. But still he descended from the helicopter behind her, silently checking her safety. It was because of the mess it would make of all his carefully constructed plans should she for any reason become unable to complete her part in their planned tour. This concern for her welfare had nothing whatsoever to do with her in any personal sense. Nothing at all.

A chauffeur-driven car was waiting to drive them the short distance from the helicopter landing pad to the hotel.

Naturally Lily had read up on the place, knowing that they would be staying there, but there were no words or photographs that could do real justice to the sparkling elegance of the rich interior of the hotel foyer, with its crystal chandelier, smooth marble surfaces and gilt furniture that seemed to give everything within it a rich golden glow.

There was no necessity for them to check in. An immaculately dressed receptionist wearing a uniform that looked to Lily as though it might have been tailored by one of Italy's foremost designers asked them to follow her, whisking them upwards and then along several corridors, faithfully decorated in keeping with the villa's history, before coming to a halt outside one of several doors in the corridor.

'We have given your guest a suite overlooking the lake, just as you requested, Your Highness,' the receptionist told Marco, opening the door and then turning back to him to ask, 'If you would like to see the suite…'

Marco shook his head, and then told Lily, 'I'll meet you downstairs in the bar in half an hour. We can run through tomorrow's schedule over dinner.'

Lily nodded her head.

'The porter will be here shortly with your luggage,' the receptionist informed Lily. 'If you require any information about anything, please ask him.'

'Thank you.' The girl had switched on the lights in the room, and although she stepped into it, Lily stayed in the open doorway, watching as the receptionist led Marco to another door at the far end of the corridor. It was crazy of her to feel so alone and abandoned—as though for some reason she needed to know where Marco di Lucchesi was in case she needed him.

She heard the click of his door closing as Marco stepped into his own room. The receptionist disappeared through a pair of doors that led to the stairs. There was nothing to keep her standing in the entrance to her own room now.

No, not merely a room, Lily reminded herself as she closed the door and went to explore her surroundings. Her suite was the size of a small apartment, and consisted of a large bedroom, a sitting room and two bathrooms. The furniture was reproduction Georgian, and the suite was decorated in toning shades of dark plum and pale grey-blue, with the bed dressed in the current boutique hotel fashion with neat piles of cushions and a carefully folded deep plum silk throw at the bottom of a padded cream bedcover. Tall glass doors opened from both the bedroom and the sitting room onto a narrow balcony just wide enough for a table and two chairs. Although she couldn't see it now that it was dark, Lily guessed that the view over the lake would be stupendous. As it was, the sight of the moonlight reflecting on the dark waters, and the myriad dancing lights from craft on the lake and buildings on its banks created an almost magical picture.

A discreet ring on the bell to her room announced the arrival of the porter with her small case. After thanking him and tipping him, Lily lifted her case onto the bed and opened it. She'd packed very carefully for this tour. For the evening she'd brought with her a fine black jersey tube-shaped skirt, which could be worn long from the waist, ruched up to make a shorter skirt, or worn as a short strapless dress. To go with it she'd brought a matching black jersey body, with three-quarter sleeves and a boat-shaped neckline, a softly draped long-line black cardigan, and a cream silk blouse. Between them she hoped that these items and the costume jewellery she had also brought with her would cover every kind of event she would be expected to attend.

For daytime she had a pair of slimline black

Capri pants, a pair of jeans, and several inter-changeable tops—along with her trench coat just in case.

For dinner tonight she intended to put the caramel-coloured dress back on and wear it with a black pashmina. Since her hair had already started to escape from its knot, and given the fact that she only had half an hour before she had to meet Marco, it made sense to simply leave it down on her shoulders.

In the bar Marco was just about to sit down to check through their itinerary for the first day of their tour, when he saw Lily approaching the entrance to the room.

She was wearing the same caramel-coloured dress she had worn for the reception, and a black wrap caught up on one shoulder with a gold Maltese cross that picked out the colour of her dress. She looked effortlessly elegant, Marco acknowledged, her hair framing the delicate bone structure of her face in softly styled natural-looking waves.

He wasn't surprised to see so many of the other occupants of the bar, both male and female, turning to give her a second look. What did surprise him, though, was that she seemed oblivious to their admiration, her manner more hesitant than confident—until she saw him, and then she straightened her back and came towards him with her chin tilted challengingly, like someone ready to do battle, he recognised grimly. No one looking at her now would associate her with that seedy studio and her even more dubious reason for being there.

Marco pushed back his chair and stood up.

'Would you like a drink or would you prefer to go straight in for dinner?'

'Straight in for dinner, please,' Lily answered him

'Very well.' A brief inclination of Marco's head brought the *maître d'* over to their table to escort them through into the restaurant

'What do you think of the place?' Marco asked her, observing the manner in which she was thoughtfully studying their surroundings.

'The decor is stunning.' Lily told him truth-fully, 'but a woman coming here for a romantic *tête-à-tête* would have to be very careful about what she wore if she didn't want to end up com-peting with so much rich adornment.'

'To the man who desires her the only clothing a woman needs is her own skin. That is far more erotic to him than anything else could be,' Marco responded.

Lily could feel her face burning from the heat Marco's words had aroused inside her. The heat *and* the desire. She was glad to be able to sit down at the table to which the waiter had shown them, glad of the room's soft lighting and the large menu she had been handed to conceal her hot face.

Behind his own menu Marco was cursing him-self for the rawly sensual images their exchange had produced inside his head. His imagination was laying them out before him in loving detail, as though answering a need within him that had demanded them. Lily lying naked against the silk coverlet of his bed, watching him, wanting

him. Her skin would be all shimmering translu-
cent perfection, fine and delicate, her nipples a
deep rose-pink, her sex covered by soft blonde
hair. Her legs would be long and slender, supple
enough to wrap tightly around him…

Marco cursed himself silently again—and her.
If this had been any other woman—if he had not
known what she really was—then he could have
dealt with the situation by taking her to bed. She
was not, after all, the first woman to arouse him,
and nor had he ever been short of eager partners
to share his bed, but he had never desired any
of them with this kind of intensity. What was
happening to him? Why couldn't he control and
banish the sensual hunger she aroused in him?

The discovery that he wasn't able to do so was
like having a deep, unbridgeable chasm open up
at his feet, leaving him vulnerable and desperately trying to cling on to what he had believed
to be a perfectly safe landscape. The discovery
was demanding answers to questions for which
there was no logical answer, stirring up things
within him he had not even known were there.

And he didn't like it. He didn't like any of it. Marco liked being able to control his responses, not have them controlling him. He liked dealing in facts and logic, not being forced to endure the uncertainty of illogical emotions. Most of all he hated the fact that Lily confused him by refusing to a stay true to type. He knew what she was, and yet she kept on exhibiting behaviour that suggested she was something else. Or that he had been wrong about her. That was impossible. Wasn't it?

The only reason he was even being polite to her was for professional reasons—because of the commitment he had made to the trust's venture. The last thing he wanted to do was spend time in her company. His pride wouldn't let him back out of accompanying her, though. That would be tantamount to admitting that he was afraid of the way she made him feel.

He put down his menu, meaning to ignore her, but against his will his gaze was drawn to her. The restaurant was full, and there were many beautiful, expensively dressed women amongst the diners, but it seemed to him that Lily had a pure elegance about her that made her stand out head and shoulders above the other women. From out of nowhere the thought formed inside his head that a man would be proud to have such a wife—educated, intelligent, beautiful and elegant. Proud? To be married to a woman he couldn't trust? A woman who hid what she really was beneath an outward image?

The waiter was hovering, waiting for Lily to give him her order.

'I'll have the *missoltini* to start with,' she told him, referring to the Lake Como speciality of small sundried fish, 'and then the risotto.' Rice had been grown in Northern Italy for centuries, and risotto was very much a dish of the area.

'I'll have the same,' Marco agreed.

When the wine waiter arrived, hot on the heels of the waiter who had taken their food order, Marco glanced at the list and asked Lily, 'How do you feel about the Valtellina? I know it's a red, and we're starting with fish, but...'

Lily laughed a natural trill of laughter for the

first time since they had met, unable to conceal her amusement. She liked the fact that Marco was consulting her rather than telling her what he thought they should drink, and she knew perfectly well why he had suggested the Valtellina.

'Leonardo drank Valtellina. If it was good enough for him then it's good enough for me,' she told him.

Marco had suspected that would be her response, which was in part why he had suggested the Valtellina in the first place.

Was that actually a small smile she could see on Marco's face, as though he was enjoying a private joke? Lily wondered. He had a good smile, warm and masculine, revealing a tantalising hint of a manly cleft in his jaw and strong white teeth. Her heart missed a beat of female appreciation of his maleness, followed by a dull, hollow feeling inside her chest. Because his smile was not for her?

She was glad of the arrival of their wine to distract her from the possible meaning behind her emotional reaction to him.

* * *

'So that's the itinerary. We'll start off tomorrow morning with a visit to Villa Balbiannello. I've arranged a private tour for you. Most of the villas we'll be visiting are not fully open to the public, as you know.'

Lily nodded her head. Marco was discussing the arrangements for the morning with her over coffee after their meal, and now he added, 'Since we've got an early start in the morning, and I've got some work to do, I'd like to call it a night— unless you want more coffee.'

Was that a stab of disappointment she felt? Of course not. Lily forced herself to shake her head and tell him firmly, 'I won't sleep if I have any more coffee.'

She ought to be tired, not strung so tightly with nervous energy. It had been a long and far from easy day, to put it mildly. The truth was that she felt as though she'd been travelling on an alien emotional rollercoaster from the first moment she had set eyes on Marco.

They had dined relatively early, the restaurant was still full and busy as they left. As they drew level with one table the stunning-looking brunette seated there with several other people, called out to Marco in a very pleased voice. 'Marco, *ciao.*'

Lily wasn't surprised to see him stop as the woman stood up to reveal a perfect hourglass figure in a cream designer dress that showed off her figure to perfection. Politely she left them to it after murmuring a brief 'goodnight', sensing that the other woman's delight at seeing Marco did not extend to her. She removed from her evening bag the plastic keycard to her suite, ready to make her way there.

In the ante-room to the restaurant a large group of people were heading towards the restaurant— fashion people from Milan's fashion week, Lily guessed expertly, easily recognising the mix of expensively suited older men, bone-thin young models, and a handful of very smart women who looked like magazine editors. She had never been comfortable around such people, reminding her as they did of her past. Her stomach was churning anxiously already, her face starting to heat up with nervous dread.

Desperate to get past them as quickly as she could, she started to skirt the group—only to be brought to shocked halt when one of the men stepped out in front of her, blocking her way. Anger, disgust and most shamingly of all stomach-gripping fear washed over her in a nauseating spine-chilling surge. He put his hand on her arm as he smiled his cruel crocodile smile at her, the familiar sour smell of his breath closing her throat against the retching movement of loathing tightening it. Anton Gillman. A man she had every reason to loathe and fear. She wanted to turn and run but she couldn't.

'Lily, what a delicious surprise—and looking so grown up as well. It's been so long. It must be—what? —twelve years?'

It was surely deliberate that he was talking to her in that adult-to-child manner she remembered so well. Because he knew what hearing it would do to her.

The temptation to correct him and tell him that

it was thirteen years was dangerously strong. She must not let him know that she even remembered, never mind knew to the exact year how long it had been.

Someone bumped into her, jolting her uncomfortably. Her keycard slipped from her hand. Immediately, before she could bend down to retrieve it, Anton released her and did so for her, carefully studying the number of the suite printed on the card before taunting her softly as he held it out to her. 'If that's an invitation...'

Horror crawled along her veins.

Almost snatching the keycard from him, she said, half choking on her loathing, 'No, it isn't. You know I would never...' She stopped speaking, not trusting herself to say any more.

The people he was with had moved on into the restaurant. She felt hot and cold, as though she was in the grip of a fever.

But instead of annoying him her rejection seemed only to amuse him, because he laughed and shook his head, shook that mane of dark coiffured hair that curled down his neck just as she remembered it

'Ah, you should never say never, my dear Lily. After all, there is a great deal of unfinished business between you and I, and it would give me a great deal of satisfaction to bring it to its proper end—especially in such an undeniably sensual setting.'

Even though she knew he would be able to see and feel the shudder that ripped through her, she couldn't control it. She was fourteen again, and he a grown man, stalking her with one thing on his mind.

'I'm twenty-seven now,' she forced herself to point out to him. The past fought inside her with the present, the child she had been with the woman she now was. 'Far too old to appeal to a man of *your* tastes.'

He was watching her with amusement, and an open sexual greed that had her only increased her panic. 'Ah, but you *do* appeal to me, Lily. You always have. They say there is an extra allure to a lost opportunity. Are you here alone?'

Lily hesitated before saying quickly, 'No.'

She had waited too long before answering him, Lily knew, and his laughter chilled her with horror. It told her that he knew how she felt.

'You're lying to me,' he told her mock disappointedly, confirming her fear. 'How delightfully erotic that you still fear me. That will add a divine extra pleasure to my possession of you. And I shall possess you, Lily, because it is what you owe me. How pleasing that you should come back into my life so fortuitously. You are staying in suite number sixteen, I see.'

From the restaurant Marco watched Lily with increasing contempt. It was plain to him that she and the man knew one another very well indeed, from the way in which they were standing so intimately close to one another. The man was mature, at least twenty years older than Lily, and well dressed in a flashy kind of way.

'Marco,' Izzie Febretti complained at his elbow, 'you are not listening to me.'

'You have a husband who I am sure will be

delighted to listen to you, Izzie,' Marco pointed out, adding, 'Please excuse me,' and then walking away from the table. A long time ago he and Izzie had been lovers. Just like Lily and the man with her? Why did that thought stab at him with such vicious fury?

'Anton,' called one of the other men from the restaurant, leaving Lily free to make her escape on trembling legs. But there could be no real relief for her now that she knew not only that he was here in the same hotel but also, thanks to her own folly, he knew the number of her suite. He had enjoyed threatening and frightening her tonight, she recognised, just as she remembered him enjoying threatening and frightening the young girls he had pursued and destroyed.

'An old friend?'

The sound of Marco's curt voice broke the dark spell of fear at seeing Anton Gillman and she spun her round to look at him.

Unable to reply, she swallowed hard and then

told him unsteadily, 'If you'll excuse me, I'm…
I'm rather tired…so I'll say goodnight.'

Without waiting for Marco to respond Lily hurried towards the lift. She was desperate to escape from the surroundings that Anton Gillman had contaminated with his presence. She had been caught off-guard by his presence and foolishly had allowed him to take advantage of her shock. He had deliberately set out to undermine and frighten her, and he had succeeded. She knew she wouldn't feel safe now until she was locked in her room, Lily admitted.

Marco watched her hurry away. She had been very impatient to go to her suite. Why? Because she had arranged to meet the man he had seen her with there? She hadn't answered him when he had asked her if he was an old friend. Was he more than merely a friend?

CHAPTER FIVE

It was just over an hour since she had left
Marco—over an hour of sitting on the edge of
her bed fully dressed, with her muscles clenched
and her gaze fixed on the locked door to her
room. Beyond that she had also locked the door
to her suite, so that she would feel safe. Only Lily
knew that she did *not* feel safe—that she could
not feel safe as long as Anton Gillman was in
the hotel.

With every minute that had passed since she
had come to her suite her fear had grown. She
had tried to apply reason to the situation, to keep
calm and remind herself that she wasn't fourteen
any more, that she wasn't a girl now and was a
woman, but it hadn't made any difference. Her
fear had continued to grow until it was out of
her control and had taken her over completely.

Anton knew which suite she was in thanks to her own clumsiness. How could she feel safe there knowing that—even with her door locked and bolted?

Lily looked at her watch. It was just gone midnight . The darkest hours of the night lay ahead of her to be got through—alone and in fear. She dared not even close her eyes because of the images she knew her memory would force her to relive. The glass doors to her balcony rattled in the breeze, causing her to start up in dread, her heart hammering into her ribs.

And then, like a tiny seed of hope pushing its way through the darkness, a new thought emerged as she remembered the dream she had had and how it had made her feel. There was one place where she would be safe. One person with whom she would be safe if only she had the courage to go to him. Marco. She would be safe with him. If she told him about Anton then she would be safe.

Refusing to give herself time to analyse the instinct driving her, never mind apply any logic to it, Lily got up off the bed, flinging open the locked bedroom door and almost running for the main door as though she was already being pursued. She stopped only to grab her bag before opening the door into the corridor and, having checked that it was empty, hurrying down its length to the door to Marco's suite.

Marco had just got out of the shower, reluctantly admitting to himself that it was a relief to be there in the solitude of his room, where he could escape from the effect Lily's presence had on his self control, when he heard the frantic knocking on his suite door—the kind of knocking that overrode logic and sent his body into immediate emergency response. It had him grabbing a towel to wrap around his hips before striding towards the door.

He wasn't sure what he had expected to see when he opened it, but it certainly hadn't been Lily. Even less welcome than her arrival was the fact that she had rushed past him and was now in his room, inside his sanctuary from the conflict she had set raging inside him.

Safety... Sanctuary... Such was the extent of Lily's relief that it was only once she was inside his suite that she took in the fact that Marco's torso and hair were damp and that all he was wearing was a towel.

Her gaze slithered and skittered as she tried to avoid looking at him and couldn't. The swift response of her senses to him momentarily distracted her from her purpose in coming to him.

Marco, a man to whom the right and the ability to control his life was something he took for granted, always chose who was allowed into his life and when. No one had ever dared to challenge that right. It had been unthinkable that they should. He was the Prince di Luchessi. No one broke the rules he had made for the way he lived his life. Until now. Until Lily had come—uninvited and unwanted—into his room. He had to struggle to come to terms with the fact that she had dared to breach his defences. His personal boundaries, like his privacy, were very important to him. People did not cross those boundaries because he did not allow them to do so. He did not want casual physical intimacy with others, because casual physical intimacy could lead to pressure for emotional intimacy. That was something he would never want or give.

His status meant that a good deal of his life was played out in public. That made the privacy he claimed for himself even more important to him. As a lover he considered it his duty to ensure that his partners found pleasure and satisfaction in his arms, but as a man he preferred to sleep alone afterwards. And now here was Lily, intruding into his personal space and looking at him as though…

Did she know what she was doing to him, looking at him like that? Marco wondered grimly. Of course she did. That was why she was doing it. He was not vain about his body—he ate healthily and kept fit without being excessive about it—but that wide-eyed look of dazed, entranced delight Lily was giving him right now, as though his was the most magnificent male form she had ever seen, would boost any man's ego. Never mind what it was doing to his body. But this was a woman who knew all about manipulating others, Marco reminded himself. Whatever Lily had come to his suite for it certainly wasn't because she had been filled with an urgent desire for him, no matter what impression she might be trying to give him right now.

'Why are you here?' he demanded stiffly. 'What do you want?'

The sound of Marco's voice broke the spell that the intimacy of his nearly naked body had spun round her, his curtness bringing Lily back to reality.

'I had to come. Seeing Anton again after so long…so unexpectedly… He knows my suite number. I couldn't stay in my room. He…' Fear and shock disjointed her words.

'Anton?' Marco checked her, and then wished that he had simply told her to leave. After all, he wanted her out of his room. He wanted her out of his *life*, he acknowledged.

'Anton…Anton Gillman.' Just saying his name made Lily shudder. Watching her, Marco

frowned, guessing, 'The man you were with earlier this evening, after dinner?'

'Yes,' Lily acknowledged.

'You gave him your room number?'

'No. I dropped my keycard and he saw it. I was
afraid that he'd come looking for me...'

'Why would he do that?'

There was a look on her face that caught him
off guard. Fear. Raw, naked fear. He could see it
in her eyes and hear it in her voice. Against his
will it touched a nerve within him. To his own
disbelief he could feel himself reacting, weakening, as she aroused in him an instinctive male
urge to take that fear from her and to protect her.

He could not and would not allow himself to
give in to that urge. He fought against it, insist-
ing, 'He must have a reason.'

Lily shuddered as Marco's words reminded her
of exactly what reason Anton did have for per-
secuting her.

Marco watched as she shuddered and a mental
image from the past was resurrected from the
place where he had buried it. Time after time

Olivia, her face swollen and bruised, had cried out emotionally to him that she wanted him to take her home, away from her latest 'boyfriend' and his physical abuse of her, and then less than twelve hours later she would be telling him that nothing and no one would ever part her from the man she loved, and that his violence towards her was simply caused by jealousy.

Some women were like that. Some women were drawn to men who abused and humiliated them. Some women even enjoyed deliberately making such men jealous, and went back time and time again to them. Was *that* why she was here? Because she knew her ex-lover would seek her out and she wanted him to believe she was with someone else?

It all made sense now, Marco decided cynically. She had come here intending to use him to make another man jealous. And she'd nearly succeeded, he was forced to admit. That knowledge caused him to state harshly, 'I know what you're up to. You came here to me because you want to make this Anton believe that you and I are lovers.'

He had hardened his heart against her now. He knew that look of fear had been faked, for all that he had initially been deceived by it. She was very good at pretence, as he had already discovered, but he was not a naive eighteen-year-old any more, ready to trust a woman just because she was a woman, ready to accept whatever lies she chose to feed him.

Lily stopped pacing to stare at him in despairing disbelief. How could he think that?

'No,' she denied. 'No, that's not true. I'm so scared—' Her body gave another violent shudder at the thought of having to endure any kind of intimacy with the man she loathed and feared so much, but Marco didn't notice. He was too caught up in the defence mechanism within him that refused to allow him to trust her.

She had come here to his room. She had looked at him as though he was the first man she had seen, the only man she wanted to see, and to his own chagrin he had responded to that look.

That was a danger he could not allow to exist. Far better and safer to destroy that response by coming to the conclusion that he had than to risk allowing his vulnerability to her. It made sense to punish himself for that vulnerability by facing up to the reality of what she was based on his own assessment of her. It was entirely logical for him to believe that she was trying to manipulate him. If there were holes in the fabric of his argument, if there were fault lines that threatened to bring it down—such as why, for instance, a chance encounter should lead to Lily being willing to stop at nothing to make an ex jealous—then he did not wish to see them.

'You're lying—again,' he insisted, in defence of his argument, and shored it up with a cold, 'But you're wasting your time. Now, if you'd be kind enough to leave, I've got some work to do.'

Without waiting for her response Marco turned his back on her and headed for the door.

Marco had got it all wrong. Panic spilled through Lily. She had to make him understand. She couldn't let him send her back to her room.

The ring of the room's telephone had him turning away from the door and crossing the room to answer the call. He was going to abandon her and leave her defenceless, undefended and unprotected, just as her father had done. She couldn't let that happen—especially when somehow she knew deep down inside herself that there was a human being who cared about the welfare of others buried deep within that inviolate image he chose to project.

He had his back to her now, as he reached for the receiver. Her heart banging into her ribs, her actions driven by the adrenaline of fear, Lily ran into the bedroom, pushing the door closed behind her with one hand. She was trembling from head to foot with the panicked need for speed, her mouth dry with anxiety as she climbed into the bed, pulling the bedclothes round her. What she really wanted to do, she recognised, was to hide herself away underneath them, to hide herself away for ever. But of course she couldn't do that. Marco's anger had showed her the contempt he felt for what he thought she was doing. Surely in view of that contempt he would leave her where she was? Lily reasoned. Rather than risk contaminating himself by touching her and physically ejecting her from his room?

She hoped so. Because if there was one thing she did know beyond all other things it was that she could not go back to her suite and stay there all alone, growing more terrified with every second that passed. Men like Anton fed off the fear of their victims. She knew that. But even knowing it she couldn't control her own fear.

The bedroom door opened. Marco stood framed in the doorway, his mouth hard with fury.

'I'm not going back to my own room,' Lily told him defiantly. 'I'm staying here. With you.'

It was those last two words that did it, setting a match to Marco's already tinder-dry fury and making it burn at a white-hot heat. How dared she lie there in his bed and calmly make it plain that she expected him to play along with her little game as though he simply didn't matter? Did she think he was completely without any male

instincts? Any male desire, any male susceptibil-
ity to the temptation she was offering?

His fury burned through his self-control.

Advancing towards her, he told her savagely,
'He must have been good.'

'What?'

'He must have been good if you are *this* desperate to get him back. Making him jealous and
getting him back is what this is all about, isn't
it?' He had reached the bed now, one hand reaching for the covers Lily had drawn up protectively
over herself.

'No, of course not. Marco, please let me stay,'
Lily begged him, desperately holding onto the
bedding.

Marco had grabbed a fistful of the fabric and
she could feel where his bunched knuckles were
grazing the upper curves of her breasts through
the layers of material. By some alchemy of their
own her nipples started to ache and tighten, and
a cord of shockingly hot sweet desire was pulling
so taut inside her that she could feel the pulse
of its beat sending out waves of awareness from

deep inside her to the sensitive nerve-endings lining the soft outer flesh of her sex. A new form of panic seized her. This wasn't what she should be feeling. Beneath the bedclothes Lily squirmed sensually, choking back a small bemused gasp at the speed with which her sensuality vied with her fear.

'Keep me safe, Marco,' she pleaded.

Marco knew his self-control was on a short rope. He could feel it straining and stretching against its tether, that dark well of male desire for her that should not be there surging savagely into life. Her breath grazed his cheek, her lips parting as she fought to resist him—to resist him because she wanted to use him, so that she could arouse within another man the jealousy she had already aroused in him.

That knowledge was all that was needed to sever his hold on his self-control.

The extent of the anger he felt at the thought of her with another man was so alien to him that it took Marco several seconds to grasp what it actually was. He was jealous? Jealous because she wanted someone else? How could that be? It could not be. But it was, Marco knew. Somehow she had conjured up from within him a version of himself he had never imagined might exist. A version of himself that was all primeval male.

The thought of those softly parted lips being possessed by another man ripped at the pride of the previously unknown version of himself she had somehow brought to life inside him. With a smothered oath Marco slid his hand along the soft column of her throat, bending her back against the pillows, telling her thickly, before his mouth closed over hers with angry male possession, 'Very well, then. If you won't leave, why don't we really give him something to be jealous about?'

Marco was kissing her, and immediately nothing else mattered. Immediately no one else mattered. Immediately she was kissing him back as her heightened emotions exploded into a surge of sensual hunger.

At some deep level inside he had known from the first minute he had set eyes on her that it

would be like this between them. He had sensed
it, felt it and tried to reject it. But now it was too
late for him to reject it, or her, any longer. He had
known that his senses and his body would take
fire from the wild sensuality of her. He had told
himself that she wasn't what he wanted. But he
had lied to himself, Marco knew. *This* was why
she had angered him—because he had known.
His hunger for her ran though him like a deep
subterranean power, possessing him and driving him. *This* was why she had angered him so
intensely—because at some level he had known
that she would take him down into this dark intensity of need where he had no control.

Beneath Marco's kiss Lily gasped and moaned.
So this was a woman's desire for the man who
could arouse that in her—this was her need and
her longing, her sensuality stripped bare of its
protection, whilst her body ached to be stripped
bare of its covering by the hands of the man
holding her. No wonder she had feared it and
tried to hide herself. No wonder she now wanted
to give herself up to it entirely and completely,

her body, her senses, her emotions—all that she offered in an almost pagan sacrifice to the man whose touch held her in such thrall.

Instinctively she clung to Marco, needing his strength to sustain her and guide her through such uncharted waters, her senses clamouring for fulfilment of the desires and needs their intimacy had unleashed. Beneath his kiss her tongue-tip hesitantly sought and found his, quickly retreating from the shock of sensation that sent a deep shudder jolting through her body, only to return to stroke against his tongue again, more slowly this time, her heart thudding erratically into her ribs as she savoured the unfamiliar intimacy.

Marco groaned beneath her exploratory touch—a sound of protest against the torment she was inflicting on him mixed with a raw need for deeper intimacy. When her tormenting caresses didn't offer it he took matters into his own hands—literally. He cupped her face, stroking his tongue against her own, his desire driving a sensual rhythm to its movement that nearly brought Lily's heartbeat to a standstill.

The rhythm of the movement of Marco's tongue against her own was the rhythm of life—the rhythm that created life itself.

The bedclothes had slipped away from Lily's body. Marco could feel the soft motion of her breasts rubbing against his bare chest through her clothes. He warned himself not to lose control, but it was too late. Ruthlessly he stripped off her dress and bra, and his body surged in an almost violent sensual reaction to the sight of the soft, shapely curves of pale female flesh, perfectly shaped and tip-tilted, with deep rose-pink nipples that right now were stiffly erect with arousal. Groaning against what he was feeling, Marco tried to fight against the desire burning through him—but the fight was already lost, because he was already reaching out to cup Lily's breasts in his hands, enticed by her open shivers of mute pleasure into driving his tongue even more deeply into the wet heat of her mouth.

How had it happened? How had she gone from abject fear to this? Lily tried to ask herself through the delirious fever that had taken possession of her.

Beneath his towel Marco could feel his body harden. His erection ached and throbbed madly, sending the blood pounding through his veins and with it the unbearable ache and heat of his desire.

Was it her release from fear that had somehow sparked off this torrent of wild female need inside her? This almost frenzied, frantic yearning for everything that Marco could give her? Lily didn't know. She just knew that the feel of his tongue against hers, the stroke of his fingers against her breasts and her nipples as he tugged erotically on their flauntingly aroused hardness, was sending her crazy with longing. Her—a twenty-seven-year-old woman who had never previously experienced the full passion of her own desire.

She reached out for Marco's body, exploring the muscles in his shoulders, blind with delight at the sensation of his flesh against her hands, stroking her way down his arms to his elbows, then up the solid, flaring V of his torso and all the way down his back, from his shoulders to the barrier of his towel. Her palms were flat against his flesh, the better for her to absorb every sensation against her own skin. Each one of her five senses clamoured to be sated. This was surely what she had been born for, what she had been created a woman for. She could feel the drumbeat of the call of her own desire driving insistently within her.

Marco could feel her hand resting on the small of his back, against the edge of the towel, and her touch was sending wrecking shudders of longing pounding through him.

His tongue twisted against hers, his mouth pressing hungry kisses against the parted softness of her lips. A kind of madness seemed to have possessed him. A voice, words he barely recognised as his own, pleaded and urged between his kisses. 'Unfasten it.'

Unfasten it and touch me. Know me as though I am the first and only man there's ever been.

'Marco…Marco…' His name slipped helplessly

from her lips, the sound a driven breath of aching need, and her fingers slipped on his arousal-slick flesh as she worked to obey his demand.

She was a sorceress, a Circe, tempting and entrancing him with the spell of her sensuality, binding him to her, trapping him in the promise of what she was offering with every touch of her hands, every arch of her back against him, every soft breath of response she gave to his touch. She was the hottest, sweetest woman he had ever touched or tasted—the only woman his body felt it could ever or would ever want to know. His desire for her drowned out every instinct that should be urging him to resist her, feeding itself on every beat of her heart against the hand that covered her breast. Her nipple rose tight and hard against his palm, calling to him to stroke its eager arousal with the pad of his thumb, to roll it between thumb and finger so that she arched up against him in wild abandon. The curve of her spine was lifting her body, offering the fruit of his own conjuring for him to take between his lips, to lick and stroke and finally suckle.

The pleasure of Marco's mouth against her breast! Such an almost unbearable pleasure that it made her cry out wildly and then lift her hands to his head to hold him against her body, leaving Marco to complete the task he had set her.

The light coming in through the still open door to the suite's sitting room burnished Marco's naked body, making him look like a living bronze, Lily thought in dazed helpless delight. Her hungry gaze was desperate to absorb every detail of him, from the muscular line of his calf upwards along the powerful strength of thighs that Leonardo himself would have ached to draw, and then higher…

In the shadows of the room the dark maleness of the body hair at the apex of his thighs sent a surge of reaction shuddering through her senses—a woman's awareness of him as a man—and her gaze was drawn to the raw potent evidence of his readiness to possess her. An impulse she would never in a thousand years have expected herself to feel had her reaching out towards him, her fingers drawn to the hot satin slickness of his flesh, her fingertips stroking down the length of its maleness.

As though in retaliation for her wanton sensuality Marco took her hands, pinning them to the mattress either side of her body with his own, leaving him free to take a slow, self-control-destroying journey of exploratory kisses over her stomach and then across her thighs, whilst her body twisted and trembled helplessly beneath his erotic pleasuring. Desire gripped her in sheets of lightning intensity, quivering surges of sharply increasing longing for his full possession of her. Behind her closed eyelids she was already feverishly imagining that final intimacy, her sex turning hot and wet with eager anticipation. Her ability to think or reason logically, to remember what it was that had brought her here, had been suspended by the demand within her for absolute capitulation to her desire.

Marco gazed down at Lily writhing ecstatically beneath him. How was it that he had reached this point, this place, where this woman held the key to all the answers to everything in his life? How was it that just by breathing, just by being, she seemed able to arouse every single one of his senses whilst feeding his desire for more of her?

'Please. Oh, please!'

Lily's sharp, staccato cry of tortured need pierced the heavy sensual accompaniment to their intimacy—the sounds of deeply drawn breathing, of an aroused body moving rhythmically against linen bedclothes, of sensual kisses pressed into flesh drawn taut with desire.

It wasn't *him* she was crying out for. It couldn't be, Marco knew.

As abruptly as though someone had thrown a bucket of cold water over him, that recognition brought Marco back to reality. Releasing Lily, he pushed himself away from her on a savage thrust of anger and revulsion, keeping his back to her. He had no need to look at her to know that she would be watching him with female triumph because he had made his vulnerability to his need for her so very clear. How had he let things get so out of hand? How had he allowed his desire for her to take him down the road to a self-destruction? And, worst of all, how had he allowed his emotions to become entangled in what should have been nothing more than an instinctive male need for sexual satisfaction?

The only comfort he could offer himself now was that at least her behaviour had confirmed what he had already suspected about her, and he need not have any more doubts that he might in some way have misjudged her. And he *had* been beginning to have those doubts, Marco admitted to himself now. He had been beginning to think and to feel...what? That making love to her would be a good idea? he derided himself caustically.

What mattered most of all right now was not making excuses for himself but making it clear to Lily that, far from allowing a need for her he should not have had get out of control, he had in fact been acting out a carefully thought out plan. His pride demanded nothing less.

Inhaling, he expelled the air he'd sucked into his lungs and told her grimly, 'Having sex with someone as a displacement activity because you can't have the man you really want might be the way things are done in the world in which you live, Dr Wrightington, but in my rather more old-fashioned world it's making yourself cheap. Having sex with another man so that you can boast about doing so to an ex-lover is several notches lower down the scale from that, and it doesn't have a name I'd like to utter in a woman's presence—even a woman like you. As a man, I warn you that if you really think having sex with me is going to persuade your ex to take you back then you don't know as much about men as you think you do,' he finished curtly, getting up off the bed.

To Lily, still trying to come to terms with the intense, agonising ache of unsatisfied desire ravaging her body, his words made her feel as though her emotions were being flayed with a whip that left them ripped and bloodied in a torment of humiliation and pain. How could she have allowed herself to be so...so aroused that nothing else had mattered more than Marco possessing her? Not even her own pride and self-worth? Her shame felt like hot tar being poured into those wounds. He had deliberately led her on, deliberately tricked and trapped her into exposing her vulnerability.

She felt sick with shock and shame, and the only defence she was able to utter was a broken, 'That wasn't supposed to happen.'

It hurt her physically inside, as well as emotionally, that he should think so badly of her—but she was in no state to explain that to him. She was too shocked by her own response to him to be able to do anything more than try to take in what *had* happened.

'You're damned right it wasn't,' Marco agreed angrily. He couldn't trust himself to say anything else to her. He couldn't trust himself to stay in the same room with her, he admitted. Because if he did stay he couldn't trust himself not to go back to her. Not to take her in his arms again and make love to her until she was as incapable of wanting any other man as he already was of wanting any other woman.

Furious with himself for that weakness, Marco

headed for the door to his suite's sitting room, acutely aware of the need to put some distance between them.

His chest felt tight with the intensity of his emotions—emotions that were totally at odds with his nature. He had never felt like this before, never imagined he *could* feel like this—possessed by the kind of raw, out-of-control male needs, thoughts and desires he had believed himself too much in control ever to know. That it was a woman like Lily who had made him feel them only made the situation so very much worse. How could he, of all men, be reduced to this by a woman he should only despise?

He looked at the closed door to the bedroom. The Marco he recognised, the Marco he had always believed himself to be, would have lost no time in going back into the bedroom and ejecting Lily from his bed, if necessary. However, the Marco he was now simply didn't trust himself to go back into that room with her—because he knew that, far from ejecting her from his bed, he was more likely to end up back in it with her. That, of course, could not be allowed to happen.

How she must be laughing at him, gloating over her hold over him. Marco paced the room, his thoughts feeding his anger, knowing that he could neither escape from it or from her—Lily—the cause of it.

In the bedroom Lily lay tensely in the bed, watching the door. Marco had been so contemptuous of her, and she couldn't blame him. What on earth had possessed her to behave in the way she had? She, of all people, who had grown up fearing a woman's need to give herself completely to the man she loved because of what it did to a woman. She who had grown up believing that sexual desire was something that at its worst led to abuse and degradation, used by one person to have power over another, and at best took from those who experienced it all control over themselves and their lives. She had always been so glad that she was immune to its call, unconcerned about discovering its allure and power.

She had felt safe in her celibate world—a world in which she could breathe the dusty air of the past instead of the high-octane air of a world she had learned to mistrust.

Anton Gillman had brought her a fear that had dominated every aspect of her life—a fear that ridding herself of her virginity the minute she was sixteen, with a boy as clumsy and untutored as she herself had been had calmed to some extent, but not banished for ever. Everything she had done in her adult life had been to keep herself safe from what she had left behind—even her choice of career. She had been too confident that she had succeeded, though. She recognised that now. Too ready to believe that she was safe from the problems she had seen sex cause in the lives of others.

The truth of that had been brought home to her now. Only minutes ago in Marco's room, in Marco's bed and in Marco's arms, she had forgotten everything she had ever learned, too aroused by her own desire for him to recognise or care about her own danger.

She wanted to creep away and hide herself somewhere like the child she had once been, hiding in the cupboard off the studio where her father had kept some of his photographic equipment. But there was no hiding place from what was within herself. Her body was still tight with longing. Shamefully, she knew that it wouldn't take much at all for her desire to be reawakened to the point where it was out of her control. Marco's single touch, his briefest kiss, would be enough to do it.

Marco! She had come here to his suite because at some deep emotional level she had felt that he represented the protection and security she had always wanted and never had. But now she knew that Marco was far more dangerous than any threat Anton might make to her.

What would she do if Marcus came to her now and took her back in his arms?

The leap of aching longing that gripped her told her all she needed to know. Not that Marco was likely to do that, of course. He had made that more than plain. But she couldn't get out of the bedroom without going into the sitting room beyond it, and she couldn't do that, Lily knew. If she did she couldn't trust herself not to humiliate herself even more by begging Marcus to take her back to bed.

An instinct she desperately wanted to ignore was trying to tell her that what had happened had *not* been a merely physical act, disengaged from her mind and her emotions. She didn't want to listen to it, and she certainly wasn't going to believe it. Yes, she had been overwhelmed—but that was just because she wasn't used to such an intensity of physical desire. Nothing more.

After all, she had seen what giving everything to one man—wanting him, needing him, loving him utterly and completely—had done to her mother when that one man had grown tired of her and wanted her out of his life. She had seen the pain of that destroy her mother emotionally, and then mentally, and finally physically—until all she had wanted was death. As a child her father had often told her that she was just like her mother. She must not let what had happened to her mother happen to her. She must not repeat her mother's mistakes.

She knew how little what had happened meant to Marco. And she must make sure that it was the same for herself—at least as far as Marco was concerned.

CHAPTER SIX

MORNING. The beginning of a new day. A joy for those who knew happiness, but a misery for those who longed to hang on to the dark hours of the night to conceal their pain, Marco acknowledged as he stood in front of the uncurtained bedroom window, looking out across the lake whilst the sun rose in the sky.

He had barely slept. He was too tall to sleep comfortably in an armchair, and besides his thoughts had been even more uncomfortable than the chair. How could he have allowed himself to be dragged into Lily's grubby, manipulative plans? His contempt for himself was now every bit as great as his contempt for her. How could he have felt any kind of desire for her? How could he have wanted her with such intensity? He had no idea what had caused last night's weakness to overtake him, but he did know that it must not be allowed to happen again.

He rubbed his jaw with his hand, grimacing at the rough feel of his stubble. He needed a shave and a shower. He also needed to get dressed. For that, of course, he needed access to his bathroom, and his clothes. He looked grimly at the closed door between the two rooms, before striding over to it and turning the handle.

Lily was lying motionless in the large bed, all that was visible of her above the bedclothes the tumble of her hair and the curve of her throat. Her body formed a slender shape beneath the covers, She was lying on her side, almost in a small tight ball, as though in her sleep she felt the need to protect herself. *He* was the one in need of protection—especially from the desire she somehow managed to arouse in him. Marco frowned. The very idea of a woman like Lily needing any kind of protection was risible, and he was a fool if he allowed himself to entertain it. Of course she no doubt would love knowing that he was vulnerable to her.

Her clothes—the clothes which last night he had discarded on the floor—were folded neatly on the chair. Marco looked briefly at them, his attention momentarily caught by the sight of her bra, half tucked away beneath her dress. He remembered now how it had struck him as he'd removed it that its plain, practical style was somehow at odds with the kind of bra he would have expected someone like her to wear. Surely something much more sexy and alluring would have been more in keeping with her lifestyle? Or perhaps, like the consummate actress she obviously was, she immersed herself so completely in her chosen part that even her underclothes had to reflect it. Dr Lillian Wrightington must not be allowed to be the kind of woman who wore sensual underwear.

He walked past the bed, the sunlight throwing his shadow across her sleeping face. Immediately her eyes opened, her head turned, the colour coming and then going in her face. Her eyes widened as she looked at him.

'Excellent,' he told her cynically. 'You've got

the "shocked, prim young woman finding a man in her room" look off to perfection. Especially after last night.'

Lily's face burned. He was talking about her passionate response to his touch. He had to be. And she had no way of denying that response or defending herself from whatever judgement he chose to make because of it.

Marco noted her flushed face. She was angry—obviously because he had refused to be taken in by her play-acting. Good.

'Sadly, excellent though your acting ability is, it was wasted on me as an audience since we both know that you knew exactly what you were doing when you came here last night,' he told her, determined to make sure that she knew he wasn't taken in by her. He might have been overwhelmed by his desire for her last night, but there was no way he was going to let her get away with using that weakness against him.

'What's the next scenario in this little drama you're concocting? Ideally, I suppose it should be the arrival of your ex-lover and his realisation that you spent the night in another man's room.'

The initial shock of opening her eyes and seeing Marco wearing only a towel and standing beside the bed looking down at her, had left Lily too stunned to speak. But now she was fully awake—and fully aware of the events of the previous evening. She had embarrassed herself and infuriated Marco. Things had been bad enough between them before, but her behaviour last night would make a workable business relationship between them virtually impossible. The last thing she wanted was Marco thinking that she was going to make unwanted advances to him. She had to assure him that that wasn't going to happen, no matter how uncomfortable that would be for her.

'I'm really sorry about last night.' she began apologetically, but with firm dignity, sitting up in the bed and making sure that the bedclothes were very firmly wrapped around her. No way did she want Marco thinking that her behaviour was sexually inviting. He had, after all, already made it clear that he did not want her when he had left her last night.

'My behaviour was totally… It was inappropriate. It shouldn't have happened. And if possible I'd like you to forget that it did happen, if you can.'

Marco's gaze narrowed. What kind of game was she playing now? Was she hoping to get him to admit that he had wanted her? Her downcast gaze and her pseudo-humble words were just a pose. That 'if you can' was definitely a challenge to him. Did she want to humiliate him with that knowledge, mock him, telling him that he couldn't resist her?

'I should have thought you would be more concerned about letting your ex-lover know that you spent the night here than with expressing regrets to me. Why don't you go and find him now?'

She opened her mouth to refute his accusation, but before she could do so the closed door between the bedroom and the suite's sitting room opened to reveal a hotel maid, her arms piled high with immaculately folded clean towels, accompanied by an older woman, obviously of more senior status, with clipboard and pen in hand. The older woman broke off speaking to the maid to cast with expert glance round the room, with Lily still in its bed and Marco clad only in a towel, before apologising and then making a swift exit.

Marco exhaled in grim irritation, only realising then that he had failed to use the 'privacy' facility for the suite the previous night.

The fact that Lily had flushed a deep pink and was looking acutely mortified and uncomfortable was lost on him as he strode across the sitting room to the suite's door to rectify his omission, coming back towards her to demand, 'What? Nothing to say?'

Lily took a deep breath. On the contrary, she had plenty to say—and she intended to say it.

'I've tried to…to apologise for last night, but it seems that rather than accept my apology you prefer to accuse me…to suggest that Anton was…'

As hard as she was trying to behave in an adult,

businesslike manner, Lily's emotions balked at using the word 'lover' with regard to Anton, so great was her fear and detestation of him.

'Was your lover and you now want to make him jealous,' Marco insisted

'No. The last thing I want is for Anton to come in search of me.'

'It's well known that hell hath no fury like a woman scorned. You've quarrelled with him and you want to make him regret that and regret the end of your relationship. You want to make him jealous. You want him to go to your room and think when you aren't there that you're with someone else—and you are prepared to use any means in order to do so. Isn't that the truth?'

'No. I would never stoop to that kind of behaviour,' she told him, her voice trembling slightly with the force of her feelings. 'I came here to you for one reason and one reason only, and that was because I was too afraid to stay in my own room.'

'Why?' When Lily looked away from him instead of answering him Marco challenged her.

'If you're as afraid of this Anton as you expect me to believe there must be a reason.'

There *was* no reason other than the one he had already suggested, Marco was sure, and that was why she couldn't answer him.

He had started to turn away from her, he the victor in their exchange and she the vanquished, when she said in a low, tense voice, 'Very well—yes, there is a reason, and it has nothing to do with me wanting Anton in my life.' A fierce shudder racked her body. 'Quite the opposite. But I can't…I can't talk about it.'

'Why not? Surely I deserve an explanation for your behaviour?'

'Behaviour for which I've already apologised.'

Lily had had enough. She could feel her self-control fraying and giving way under the pressure of her emotions. She bent her head, not wanting Marco to realise how close to the edge she was, how afraid she was that her own actions as much as her words might inadvertently give her away.

'There's no law that says I have to provide you

with an explanation of my…of the reasons for what I did as well,' she told him fiercely. 'A…a compassionate man—a man who understands and accepts that other people can sometimes be vulnerable and in need—would know that. But you aren't that kind of man, are you? You're the kind of man who wants to think the worst about others.'

'I'm the kind of man who knows when he's being lied to, if that's what you mean,' Marco agreed acidly, defending himself against the knowledge that he had been far more affected by Lily's outburst than he should have been.

'But you are *not* being lied to,' Lily insisted. 'Perhaps I should be the one questioning you about your motives for refusing to believe me rather than the other way around,' she added perceptively.

Marco felt his heart thud heavily into his chest wall. His glance fell on his watch and his heart gave a surge of relief as he saw his means of escape from what had now become a very dangerous situation.

'It's nearly eight o'clock,' he told her, ignoring her comment, 'and we're due to leave at nine.'

Seated in the privately hired hovercraft next to Marco, Lily warned herself that she was here in Italy to work, and that she must put aside the temptation to let the pressure of her secret thoughts and emotions stop her from doing that. Even though Marco's unjust accusations had hurt her as well as angered her.

After leaving Marco's suite earlier, she had only just made it downstairs in time for the arrival of their transport, having returned to her own suite first, to shower quickly and then change into jeans and a tee shirt, worn underneath her faithful cardigan.

They'd been driven to the first villa on Marco's list, where they'd been given a private tour of its art collection. After lunch at a small, elegant restaurant, where Lily had still been too wrought up by the events of the morning to do her pasta justice, they had gone on to their second villa, where Lily had discussed the loan to the trust of part of a collection of letters written to past owners of the villa by an Englishman who had stayed there in the decade following Napoleon's defeat. The third son of a duke, the Englishman had come to the lakes for his health, and the letters had been written to a young female relation of the family on his return to England as part of his courtship of her. In addition to the letters there were also some sketches he had done for her of his home in Yorkshire.

Aidan Montgomery had died from his tuberculosis before they could marry, and as she'd inspected the documents closely Lily had wondered if the marks on them came from tears cried over the letters by the fiancée he had left behind.

It had been Marco who had noticed her concentration on the stains, and Marco too who had pointed out dryly to her, when she'd voiced her thoughts, that if Teresa d'Essliers had grieved for her fiancé that grief had not stopped her from marrying someone else within eighteen months of his death.

'A diplomatic family marriage,' the curator

had told them. 'Her father was a banker who enjoyed gambling with other people's money. Her husband was one of his clients—a wealthy silk merchant who wished to improve his own social status.'

'Will we have time to visit any of Como's silk mills?' Lily asked Marco now, as the hovercraft took them to their next appointment—a villa situated at the side of the lake, with its own landing stage.

Como had been a centre for the production of silk for many centuries. Although the business was now in decline from its heyday, because of the expense of its manufacture compared with silk imported from China, it still produced many of the exclusive silks used by both interior and fashion designers.

'Do you want to visit one?' Marco asked her. His voice was curt as he focused on keeping as much emotional distance between them as he could.

The coldness in his voice made Lily flinch inwardly, but she refused to let him see how she felt, saying as calmly as she could, 'I'd like to. It could help with the exhibition.' When he looked questioningly at her, she explained, 'One of the things we're trying to do with the exhibition is interest a younger audience, and I feel that the more personal detail we can display, the more able they will be to relate to it. I thought that Como's silk business would appeal to them. I have to admit that I'd also love to see something of the archives of those companies who have been producing silk for several centuries. Although it isn't my specific field, I've seen some of the work that's being done on the research and restoration to the decor of the trust's properties, and some of those fabrics are just so beautiful.'

'I'm surprised you haven't mentioned Como's silk industry's connection with the modern-day fashion industry. Surely that would have an even greater appeal to you, with your own involvement in that particular business?'

'What do you mean? What involvement?' Lily's voice was sharp with anxiety.

'I was referring to your other means of

income—the photographic studio,' Marco reminded her grimly.

Lily's body almost sagged with relief. For one awful moment she thought that somehow Marco had guessed about her past and her father.

'I've already told you,' she defended herself, 'I was doing a favour for…for someone.'

'That someone being a man, I assume?' Why was he doing this to himself? Why was he deliberately feeding his own jealousy like this? Prior to Lily coming into his life, if asked, Marco would have said and believed that he was not a man who felt jealousy. He had certainly never experienced it with any of his lovers.

But he was experiencing it now, and it galled him like a thorn sticking into his flesh that Lily should be the person to inflame his feelings to such a pitch, to such a destructive emotion. She represented so much that filled him with contempt it should have been impossible for him even to want her, never mind feel about her as he did.

'Yes,' Lily was forced to admit.

If only she had not agreed to help her half-brother. If only she and Marco had met for the first time at the reception and not at that wretched studio. Then what? Then he would have taken one look at her and yearned for her? Was that what she had done? Had she taken one look at him and somehow known what was to happen to her and that she would want him? A deep shudder tormented her body.

What had caused her to look like that? Marco wondered. So...so *stricken*, somehow, as though she was having to face a terrible, inescapable truth? She was simply trying to arouse his pity, he warned himself. She was, after all, an excellent actress—as he had good cause to know.

Lily took a deep breath, reminding herself that she was a qualified professional with a job to do. She couldn't let herself be hurt even more. All she could do was try to protect herself by pretending that nothing untoward had happened.

'Is that the villa we're approaching now?' she asked Marco, in what she hoped was a calm and businesslike voice.

Marco had to bend his head to look out of the window of the hovercraft, his action bringing him far too close to her for Lily's comfort, making her feel as though she had jumped from one uncomfortable situation into another that was every bit as uncomfortable in a different way. With him this close to her she could smell the clean tang of Marco's soap mixed with the sensual warmth of his body. The hovercraft jolted on the movement of the water, forcing her to lean as far back as she could to avoid coming into physical contact with him. After what had already happened she couldn't bear to have him thinking that she was tempted to take advantage of the opportunity to be close to him.

Men soon tired of women who were too vulnerable to them. They preferred the excitement and the challenge of the chase, the power of winning their trophy. When that trophy became needy and dependent they no longer wanted it. She had seen that so often with her father. She had seen it break her mother's heart and spirit. Better not to love at all than to be destroyed by the pain of loving someone who had grown bored and become indifferent to you.

A strand of hair had escaped from the clip Lily had used to secure it into a soft knot away from her face, and Marco had an aching urge to reach out and lift it from her skin. If he did his knuckles would graze the soft flesh of her throat and she would turn and look at him, her grey eyes dark and questioning, her lips parted for his kiss. He wanted that to happen, Marco recognised on a savage stab of brutal self-knowledge. He wanted to take her in his arms right now and hold her. He wanted to kiss her until she murmured his name against his mouth in a soft plea of arousal and need.

What was happening to him? How could he feel like this about her when everything he knew about her told him that at best he should be wary of her and at worst he should despise her? Earlier in the day, watching her as she'd talked to the curators of the two villas they had visited, listening to her as she spoke with them, he had seen a woman who was a skilled communicator, a woman who knew and loved her subject and who wore her knowledge comfortably, a woman who had been willing to listen respectfully to what the curators had to tell her even when Marco suspected she was far more knowledgeable about the collections and the history of the villas than they were themselves—a woman, therefore, to whom the feelings of others was important. And yet at the same time she was also a woman to whom the vulnerability of a foolish young man was simply something to be exploited—for money. A woman who was selfish enough to think nothing of using other people to pursue her own desires.

'Yes, it is the villa,' he confirmed as the craft headed for the landing stage. 'I've arranged for the car to pick us up from here after we've viewed the collection. I don't think there'll be time for us to visit a silk mill today. The Duchess will be expecting us, and like most people of her generation punctuality is important to her. She loves entertaining, and I wouldn't be surprised if she's made arrangements to that effect for this evening—probably for a dinner party. However, if you'd rather not be involved, I'll have a word with her and tell her that you have work you want to catch up on. I expect you will have reports you want to file with the trust.'

She did, it was true, but Lily suspected his suggestion sprang more from his wish not to have to endure any more of her company than he had to rather than any concern for her.

'There's no need for you to do that. Being involved with the villa owners is part of my job. Besides, I imagine that the Duchess has some fascinating stories to tell about her family history and the villa. However, if that is a polite way of telling me that you don't want me there...?' she challenged Marco, determined to let him know that she had guessed the real reason behind his offer.

'It isn't,' he denied. 'I merely thought you might wish to have some time to yourself.'

'I'm here to work. And that work includes listening to what those connected with the villas have to say,' Lily told him firmly.

* * *

It was a little later than Marco had allowed for on their schedule before they were able to leave the third villa. It had been in the same family for several generations, having originally been built for one of Napoleon's favourite generals, and in addition to agreeing to loan the trust several valuable pieces for its exhibition the owner, an elderly Italian who spoke impeccable English, had allowed Lily to take photographs of the interior of the villa, which would also be put on display—a coup indeed, as she was fully aware.

Watching Lily with her camera, Marco could see her professionalism—but instead of admiring it, as did the Visconte, whom she had charmed completely with her interest in his family history, her expertise brought back all Marco's doubts about her and his disdain for what he believed she was.

He would be glad when this task was over and he could return to his normal life and put Dr Lillian Wrightington out of his mind for ever. And out of his heart? The sneaky little question was slid under his guard so dextrously by that taunting inner voice he literally stopped in mid-stride as he fought to deny the unjustifiable allegation. She meant nothing to him. Nothing, that was, apart from the fact that he didn't trust her and last night she had aroused him to the point where nothing had been more important than possessing her. So he had desired her? Physical desire alone meant nothing. His emotions weren't engaged with her. That was impossible. Wasn't it?

Then how did he explain away his anger and jealousy?

Marco welcomed the distraction from his inner thoughts provided by the necessary formalities involved in taking their leave of the Visconte and thanking him for his kindness.

As their chauffeur-driven car purred up the drive to the Duchess's home, through the most beautiful formal Italianate gardens, Lily was uncomfortably conscious of Marco's silence. He had barely spoken to her since they had left the previous villa, and she had felt too aware of coldness of the stone wall of his silence to want to break it.

The front of the elegant Palladian-style villa was basking in the last of the early October sunshine beneath a clear blue sky, and as always when she was in the presence of a beauty that stirred her senses Lily felt her emotions rise up in humble awe. It didn't make any difference to her reaction if it was nature that was responsible for that beauty or the skill of a human artist—the effect on her was the same.

Unable to stop herself, she murmured more to herself than Marco, 'This is just so beautiful.'

Somehow the emotion in Lily's voice managed to find a faint hairline crack in Marco's defences that he hadn't known was there. The moisture he could see glinting in her eyes couldn't possibly have been faked, he knew, even though he wanted to believe that it was. A fresh surge of jealousy spiked through him—but not over another man this time. 'Both the setting and the villa do please the eye,' he told her in a dry voice. 'But I like to think that my family's *castello* can rival the villa for catching at the heart. You'll have to give me your opinion when you've seen it.'

The di Lucchesi *castello*. The place from which Marco's family sprang. The place where his ancestors would have taken their wives and sired their children. Children. Lily's heart rocked perilously inside her chest, pierced by an agonised ache of pure female longing and envy. One day Marco would take a bride to his *castello*, and one day she would give birth to his child, his children there. But that woman would not be her. What was she doing, allowing herself to accept thoughts and feelings that could only cause her pain and make her suffer? That mattered to her? Then that must mean...

Lily didn't want to think about what it could mean. It was a relief when the car came to a halt and she knew that she'd soon be able to escape from Marco's presence and the effect he was having on her.

The Duchess herself came down the stone steps leading up to the villa to greet them, welcoming them with warm smile before telling the chauf-feur that her housekeeper had a meal ready for him, if he wanted to drive round to the courtyard at the back of the villa.

Such kindness and concern was not always displayed by those in the Duchess's elevated social and financial position, Lily knew, and her heart warmed even further to their host-ess as she slipped her arms through both Lily's and Marco's, telling them as they headed for the steps, 'There's no need for the two of you to be bashful or feel you have to be discreet.' She pulled a face and laughed. 'All that creeping around in the middle of the night, terrified that one might step on a creaking floorboard and be discovered. I remember it well. But times have changed, and I like to think that I have changed with them. So, once my housekeeper informed me that her sister—who works at Ville d'Este— had told her the two of you had been sharing a room there, I instructed her to make up my fa-vourite guest suite for the two of you.'

CHAPTER SEVEN

LILY couldn't speak. She couldn't even think properly. She couldn't do anything other than look at the Duchess in mute disbelief as she continued, 'I'm sure you'll like it. It has the most wonderful view over the lake. My late husband and I used to stay in it when we came to visit before my father died. When I inherited it my husband insisted that we replace the rather small double bed with something larger and more comfortable.' The Duchess gave a fond sigh. 'I have so many happy memories of being young here. New love—it is so special. I well remember the first time I saw my late husband. I fell in love with him the minute I set eyes on him. He, though, I'm afraid to say, did not return my feelings for a full twenty-four hours after we had met,' she told them drolly, adding, 'I hope that your brief stay here will give you both some memories that you too will come to cherish.'

All the time she had been talking ~~them~~ they had been climbing the steps. Now they had reached the top, and Lily's heart was pounding— but not because of any exertion involved. Had she understood the Duchess correctly? Had she instructed her housekeeper that she and Marco were to share a bedroom—and a bed? Lily tried to look at Marco, but the Duchess was linked between them, beaming first at Marco and then at Lily, obviously very proud of what she had done and no doubt thinking she was doing them both a favour.

'I have to say, Marco,' the Duchess continued blithely, 'I think that Lily is the perfect girl for you. You both feel so passionately about Italian art and history, and my late husband always used to say that shared interests remain a strong bond between a couple long after the first flush of romance has faded. Ah, good—here we are. Do come in and admire my ancestors, Lily. I hope I may call you Lily? After all we are practically family already, since Marco and I are distantly related.'

The villa's hall was round, with a wonderful balustrade stairway rising exactly opposite the front door then branching off to form a round gallery landing. The design was repeated on each of the three floors, so that it was possible to look up from the ground floor and see the stained glass dome of the cupola several floors above them.

'When the sun is overhead, the light from the stained glass makes the most magical patterns. When we were children my brother invented a game whereby we had to chase the moving pattern of a certain colour all the way up and down the stairs. He was older than me, and he always won. He should have inherited the villa, of course, but he was killed during the Second World War. He was only nineteen.'

Lily was listening to the Duchess, but at the same time she was tense with inner anxiety as she waited for Marco to explain to her that there had been a mistake and they were not a couple.

Only he said nothing, and now the duchess was exclaiming, 'Ah, here is my housekeeper, Berenice. She will show you to your room. I hope you don't mind, but I have taken the liberty of organising a small reception here tonight. Just some old friends I know will enjoy meeting you, Lily. They all have connections with the area and its villas, so don't be shy about asking them any questions you may have. We'll meet again in the main salon.'

Their room.

Lily gave Marco an imploring look but still he said nothing, and continued to say nothing until they were alone in the villa's best guest suite. Lily asked him anxiously why he had not corrected the Duchess's misapprehension about their relationship.

'If you had not come to my room last night we would not be in this situation.'

Marco's uncompromising statement couldn't be denied, but Lily still shook her head as she paced the elegant suite. Marco stood in front of one of the room's long sash windows, his head turned so that he was half looking out across the lake and half looking back into the room.

'I know why the Duchess thinks that we are a couple, but you could have told her the truth. You could have explained to her...'

'I could have explained what? That you came to my room seeking to use me—either to protect you from your ex or to make him jealous? Is that really what you would have wanted me to say to her?'

Without giving her the chance to answer, Marco gave a dismissive shake of his head, telling her grimly, 'Anyway, she likes you. She wouldn't believe me.'

He didn't have to say that he neither understand nor shared the Duchess's feelings. The tone of his voice said it for him.

She mustn't allow herself to feel hurt yet again, Lily warned herself. But it was too late. The pain was already flooding through her.

'She's a romantic,' Marco continued. 'She would simply think that I was trying to hide our relationship from her.'

'We haven't *got* a relationship,' Lily told him. Tears were threatening to clog her throat.

'The Duchess believes that we have. And not just a sexual relationship. She's managed to convince herself that we've fallen in love with one another.' The derision in Marco's voice made Lily's face burn. 'If she knew you rather better, of course, she'd know that was impossible.'

Lily swallowed on the misery his caustic comment brought her.

'No. We can't say anything to her,' Marco told her. 'For her own sake. Were we to insist to her now that there isn't a relationship it would result in either her not believing us or in her embarrassment for misjudging the situation if she does believe us. Neither of those situations is acceptable to me. It will make things easier all round if we simply accept the situation as it is. After all, we're only here for two nights.'

'Two nights!' She couldn't share a room and a bed with him for two nights, feeling the way she did about him. 'What if sharing a room with you isn't acceptable to *me*?' she demanded.

Marco turned round fully to look at her.

'Do you really expect me to believe that after last night?' he challenged her. 'After all, you didn't have any objection then—in fact it was what you wanted.'

Lily's heart missed a beat. Was Marco hinting that he knew there had been a time last night when what she had wanted from him had been much more personal and intimate than merely the protection of his presence? She hoped not. It was humiliating enough that *she* knew how she felt about him, without the added humiliation of having to deal with the fact that he knew as well.

'That was different,' she defended herself, adding emotionally in her growing panic, 'I don't *want* to share a room with you.'

'Do you think I want to share one with you?' Marco asked her grimly. 'You are the one who is primarily responsible for the situation we now find ourselves in, not me. I suppose I should have expected this kind of selfishness from you. After all, a woman who tries to use one man to make another jealous has to be innately selfish.'

She could tell him the truth. She could make him feel thoroughly ashamed of himself for the way he was misjudging her, Lily knew. But it was clear he only wanted to believe the worst of her, and she was not about to tell him her darkest, most painful secret only to have him coldly dismiss her as an accomplished liar.

How could she have allowed herself to become entangled—trapped—in this situation? She knew where her vulnerabilities lay. She knew where she was weak. If she'd thought more carefully and clinically about the way he had made her feel that first time she had seen him at the studio, she could have… She could have what? Walked away from the work she had been paid to come here and do when she'd recognised him at the reception? When she prided herself on her professionalism? Hardly.

'I will not have the Duchess embarrassed or upset by you causing a dramatic fuss about something that, after all, means very little in this day and age,' Marco warned her. 'And who knows? If your ex gets to hear about it perhaps it will have the desired effect and bring him back—although as a man I'd have to caution you against encouraging a man to be jealous. It makes for a relationship based on distrust, and no man who values himself can or should compromise where trust is concerned. That can be very dangerous.'

'You sound as though you're speaking from experience.' The words were out before Lily had time to think about what she was saying.

Their effect on Marco was immediate. What was it about her that led to him revealing things about himself to her—private, fiercely guarded things he would never normally dream of revealing to anyone. His face hardening, his voice chilling, he told her, 'I've certainly got enough experience to know not to trust *you*.'

Lily flinched, stung by his icy words. She hadn't lied to him, but he had made it plain that he had no intention of believing her. Had he in the past been hurt by someone—a woman he'd trusted who had lied to him—and now he refused to trust any woman? He must have cared a great deal for her, whoever she was. A very great deal. The man he was now wouldn't let any woman close enough to do that to him. A horrible feeling of desolation sucked the strength from her. It was stupid, foolish, self-destructive of her to care because Marco had once loved someone so much.

Marco frowned. Why was Lily looking so stricken? She'd been perfectly happy to share a room—and a bed—with him when it had suited her. Now she was looking as though the very thought of doing so was destroying her, and she was obviously rejecting it—and him—in favour of another man. Any sympathy Marco might have been tempted to feel for her vanished.

'Do you understand?' he demanded.

Blindly Lily looked at him. He might not have any compassion for her, but obviously the Duchess's feelings were important to him, so there must be some humanity within him some-where—even if he seemed intent on concealing it from her.

'Yes, I understand,' she confirmed emotion-lessly.

She understood that he loathed and despised her. She understood that there had been a woman in his life who had destroyed his ability to trust. But what she did not understand was why her silly heart persisted in aching with a need that could only destroy her. And tonight she was going to have to share a room with the cause of that need and somehow keep it hidden from him. If she could.

But what if she couldn't?

What if, like the last time she had shared a bed with him, she let her feelings get out of control? Panic filled her.

'We can't share a room,' she insisted. 'I wouldn't feel...'

'What? Safe?' Marco derided her.

Lily couldn't look at him—dared not look at him just in case he could somehow see what she was really thinking. The truth was that she was indeed afraid that she wouldn't feel safe. Not because she was afraid that she couldn't trust Marco, but because she feared that she couldn't trust herself. She certainly wasn't prepared to admit that to him, though.

'I've just told you we have no other option than to be thankful that it's only for a couple of nights,' Marco said, adding sardonically, 'Allow me to play the gentleman and offer you the bed.'

He wasn't going to be persuaded or argued into changing his mind about the suite, she could tell. And in reality what legitimacy did she actually have to keep on trying to insist that he did so? She liked the Duchess herself, and knew that Marco's comment about her potential embarrassment was justified. She was going to have to accept the fact that, despite her misgivings and her fears they would be sharing the suite, she acknowledged.

'You have the bed this time,' Lily muttered. 'I'd rather have the sofa in the sitting room.'

A brief knock on the door had Marco going over to open it to admit the housekeeper, escorting a young man who was carrying their luggage.

'If there's anything you require for the evening,

just dial ten on the telephone on the desk,' she told them.

It was Marco who tipped the young man, whilst Lily was still looking round for her handbag, his gesture winning him an approving look from the housekeeper before the two of them exited the room.

'We've got just over an hour before we're due downstairs for the Duchess's reception. Since the suite seems only to have one bathroom, you can use it first if you wish,' he offered distantly, without looking at her.

Lily nodded her head. She wanted to wash her hair, and although it was easy to dry and style it would take her longer to get ready than it would Marco, so it made sense for her to use the bathroom first.

Even so, she didn't linger under the shower, washing her hair and herself as quickly as she could before pulling on one of the luxurious bathrobes provided for their use. She'd taken her small case into the bathroom with her, hanging up her black jersey skirt to make sure it wasn't creased, and was just straightening up, having removed clean underwear from her case, when there was a sharp knock on the door.

Still holding her undies, she opened the door.

'I just wanted to check that you don't need anything ironed,' Marco told her.

'No. My skirt is jersey,' Lily replied, half gesturing towards the sliver of matt black fabric hanging on the glass door of the shower area, not realising until Marco bent down to retrieve them that her briefs had slipped out of her grasp.

Pink cheeked with embarrassment, Lily took them from him when he handed them to her, balling the nude fabric in her hand as she did so. Why, when she preferred and always wore plain, smooth underwear, was she suddenly now wishing that what Marco had retrieved for her had been something far more sensual? A pretty, feminine wisp of silk and lace, perhaps—the kind of underwear worn by the kind of women she imagined Marco preferred. Beautifully, sexually confident and alluring women for whom it was second nature to dress their bodies in provocative sexy undies.

'I'll be finished in here in five minutes,' she told Marco, pointedly looking at the door.

Nodding his head, he stepped back so that she could close it.

Why had Lily been so embarrassed about him seeing her underwear, Marco wondered as he waited for the bathroom. It was illogical, given what he knew about her. Illogical and out of character for any woman of her age, never mind the kind of woman she was. Another act? If so, why? It wasn't something she could use to bait her ex.

Against his will Marco recognised that something about her reaction, coupled with the plain neatness of that pair of nude briefs she had tried to conceal in her hand, had challenged his assessment of her. Why? And why should he care if it had? He cared because somehow she had activated a rebellion within him he hadn't previously known could possibly exist—a dangerous, unwanted rebellion that wanted to overthrow the laws he had laid down about refusing to give people the benefit of the doubt, about distrusting them instead of trusting them. That rebellion was now allowing emotion to get a foothold within him. That rebellion was now constantly challenging his logic and experience. It was urging him to break his own rules. And, worse, it had joined forces with his natural male desire, and together they were trying to undermine the fortifications that protected him. Together they provoked and taunted his beliefs—beliefs he knew to be true. Together they whispered to him that it wouldn't hurt to allow himself to enjoy the pleasure that intimacy with Lily would bring.

He must not allow them any freedom.

'The bathroom's free now. I'll finish getting dressed in the sitting room.' Lily took care not to look directly at Marco as she hurried past him with her case and her skirt, her body firmly wrapped up in its bathrobe. In a household as well organised as this one was she was pretty sure there would be a hairdryer in one of the dressing table drawers, but right now, whilst Marco was safely out of the way in the bathroom, the first thing she intended to do was get dressed.

The smooth line of her long skirt and the boat-necked top she was wearing with it proved the sartorial wisdom of her smooth nude underwear, Lily tried to comfort herself five minutes later, as she studied her reflection critically in the full-length bedroom mirror. With just this kind of event in mind she had brought with her two very definite pieces of statement jewellery—a wide collar of beaten silver that lay perfectly against her collarbone, and a silver cuff that went with it. She had come across them in Florence, when she had been there on business. She had fallen in love with the jewellery on sight, and she hadn't been surprised when the young girl who had made it had told her that she had been inspired by an exhibition of Saxon jewellery she had seen in England.

Lily found a hairdryer, as she had expected, in one of the dressing table drawers, turning her head upside down so that she could blow her hair dry quickly from the roots. She had just finished doing so when Marco walked back into the bedroom, wearing a towelling robe.

Lily could feel her skin overheating again. Why? She was no stranger to the naked male body in all its artistic forms, and Marco was far from naked. *The* naked male body, perhaps, but not *this* male body. Not Marco's male body. It was ridiculous for her to feel so oddly breathless and aware of him. She had spent last night in his bed, after all. This was different, though. This sharing of a room whilst they got ready together was a very specific intimacy that was doing things to her senses and her emotions that filled her with an aching emotional yearning. For intimacy with a man—any man? For the kind of relationship with a man that provided that intimacy? Or for that intimacy and that relationship only with Marco?

The hairdryer slipped out of her grasp and fell to the floor. As she reached for it so did Marco, their hands touching. For a second neither of them moved. If they were really a couple, and really intimate, instead of removing his hand from hers Marco might have removed the hairdryer instead, before going on to take her in his arms. A bolt of shocked delight jolted through her body, causing her hand to shake as she struggled to grip the hairdryer.

'We've got fifteen minutes,' Marco told her, his breath warm against her forehead as he bent towards her. His words caused her to jerk upright, her eyes widening, before logic warned her that he was simply reminding her of when they needed to be downstairs—not suggesting to her that they had fifteen minutes in which to attempt to quench the sensual desire that had started to pulse inside her, conjured up into life out of nowhere by her own thoughts.

It was discomfiting to realise that there could be so much hidden sensuality in even the most straightforward of comments for a person whose senses and body yearned for that sensuality.

'I'm almost ready,' Lily managed to tell him. Almost ready to go downstairs, but completely and utterly and eagerly ready to stay right here and be made love to by him.

Stop it at once, she warned herself. She was behaving as though… As though she had forgotten everything she had ever learned—as though she had no concern whatsoever for her own future emotional security and peace of mind.

Standing up, she swept her hair back off her face, securing it with a neat band before twisting it into a sleek knot from which she pulled a few soft loose tendrils, all without needing to look in the mirror. She only realised that Marco had been watching her when she turned to see him looking at her.

'What's wrong?' she demanded anxiously.

Her father had always been very critical of her mother's appearance. As a little girl Lily had often watched her mother getting ready to go to parties, and she could remember how her father's comments had often resulted in a row that ended up with her mother refusing to go out. Criticising the woman they purported to love was a trick used by some men to control that woman's self-confidence and make her all the more dependent on him, and she despised herself for allowing herself to be affected by Marco's amusement now. It was too late, though, to retract her question

'Nothing's wrong,' Marco answered her curtly. As though the admission was being dragged from him, he continued, 'I was just thinking how easy you made that look.' He paused, and then, as though the words were being spoken of their own volition rather than his, added, 'And how very beautiful you look.'

Marco looked almost as shocked by the fact that he had paid her a compliment as she was herself. Lily swallowed hard, her own voice husky as she responded.

'Thank you.' His admission deserved an admission of her own from her. 'My father would never have said that to my mother. I don't think I ever heard him tell her she was beautiful, even though she was—' She broke off, shaking her head.

'Your father?' Marco questioned, causing Lily

to retreat back into her normal reticence about her background. She had said too much. She shook her head.

'My mind was wandering, I'm afraid. Silly of me. And now we've only got ten minutes. I'll leave the bedroom to you, so that you can get dressed. I can finish getting ready in the sitting room.'

She was gone before Marco could stop her to pursue the matter further, and she had been right. They did only have ten minutes left.

He joined Lily in the sitting room with three minutes to spare, looking so formidably hand-some and male in a dark suit worn with a dark blue shirt with a fine white line and a toning tie that Lilly felt herself flooded with conflicting emotions. He filled her with a desire she had never expected to feel, but at the same time he also filled her with anxiety and dread because of that desire.

Lily looked like a pagan princess, Marco thought, and a shocking of the surge of posses-sive wanting filled him, seized him, at the sight of her in her plain black outfit adorned with that almost barbarically splendid jewellery.

There would be women here this evening who would be wearing family heirloom jewellery worth a fortune, but it would be impossible for them to outshine the dramatic simplicity of Lily's appearance. Any man would be proud to stand at her side. And any man would ache for the evening to be over so that he could have her all to himself. Was that how he felt? Possessive and bitterly jealous because she preferred someone else?

Lily's, 'We're going to be late,' had him nodding his head and then going to open the door for her.

They reached the main salon—a large double-aspect room, decorated very much in the French Empire style in shades of rich gold and French blue, with two enormous chandeliers throwing out brilliant prisms of light—only seconds ahead of the Duchess's guests. There was no more time than to accept a glass of chilled champagne from one of the several formally attired waiters starting to circulate around the room.

Introduced by the Duchess to a dozen or more of her guests within as many minutes Lily was soon struggling to keep a mental note of their names. However, she wished that all she had to bear was that awkward confusion when the Duchess called Marco over to join them and then began introducing them virtually as a couple.

Since he obviously already knew some of the guests Lily expected Marco to do something to correct this error, but he did nothing about it at all, instead staying at her side whilst the Duchess beamed with obvious pride in having 'outed' their relationship. He was obviously very fond of the Duchess, and determined not to embarrass her by revealing the truth in public, Lily recognised. Whilst she could understand that, it certainly didn't make her position any less difficult to bear. Having Marco behave as though they were indeed a couple, having him standing so close to her, adopting a protective manner towards her that she knew was fictitious, brought her to a sharply keen knife-edge of painful awareness of just how much the inner vulnerable core of her longed to have the right to this kind of closeness with him.

Of course he was sophisticated and urbane enough to carry off their supposed relationship with cool self-confidence. He was that kind of man—totally at home in his surroundings and totally in control of himself. And of her? She had known him for less than a handful of days but in that time he had changed not just her beliefs about what she wanted out of life, but her perception of herself as well.

When she was confronted by the feelings aching through her now she came face to face with a part of herself she had thought locked away for ever. Somehow, though, despite it being pushed away, ignored by her and denied, Marco had the power to bring it to life within her. There was no point, though, in indulging in hopeless, self-destructive daydreams and fantasies. Lily knew that loving Marco was dangerous for her and could only bring her misery and pain.

'You need a fresh glass of champagne. That one's gone flat, by the looks of it.'

Marco was holding out a fresh glass to her and smiling as he did so. A faked smile, of course—how could it not be?—but her heart couldn't help yearning and wondering what it would be like to have Marco *really* smile at her like that, with a smile that was full of tenderness and more than a hint of sensual promise of the pleasure that would be theirs once they were on their own. A lover's smile, in other words.

Her hand trembled as she reached for the glass he was holding out to her. To disguise her vulnerability she took a quick sip of it, almost choking on the bubbly liquid in shock when she felt a hand on her arm and heard a familiar female voice exclaim, 'Lily—little Lily! Darling girl, you look *so* like your dear mother. I'd have recognised you anywhere. I couldn't believe it when I saw you. I had to ask Carolina to bring me over.'

Somehow Lily managed to smile back at the elegant mature woman now standing with the Duchess, smiling at her.

'I could hardly believe it myself.' The Duchess laughed. 'There I was, telling one of my closest friends about Marco's lovely new girlfriend and the exhibition she is organising, and when I pointed you out what should Melanie say but that she recognised you? She knew you as a little girl but lost touch with you.'

Lily was acutely conscious of Marco standing next to her, listening to everything that was being said. If there was anything that could cause her even more emotional distress and dread than recognising how vulnerable she was to Marco then it was this. Someone from her past with its memories that she had fought so hard to leave behind her.

Marco could see how shocked Lily was. Shocked in a way that suggested she had been dealt some kind of almost physical blow. She was trying hard not to show it, but he had heard her indrawn agonised breath and seen the colour leaving her face. Why? Because the Duchess's friend had known her as a little girl? *Why?*

She was trapped, Lily thought helplessly. She

couldn't simply turn and run away, no matter how tempted she was to do just that. It wouldn't have been so bad if Marco hadn't been with her. She would still have felt shocked. She would still have felt the pain that seeing Melanie had brought her. But that pain would have been much easier to bear without Marco's presence.

And now, instead of running somewhere to hide, she had to smile as though she meant it and say with as much composure as she could to the woman standing with the Duchess, 'Melanie, how lovely to see you again.'

Melanie Trinders had been a close friend of her mother. They had modelled together, and Melanie had been a regular visitor to their home.

Lily had tried to sound cool and slightly remote, but her attempt to put some emotional distance between them had no effect whatsoever on her mother's old friend. Lily was immediately embraced—wrapped, in fact—in the warmth of expensive cashmere and even more expensive scent, and subjected to a fond continental exchange of kisses before being held at arm's length by the elegant and still beautiful late middle-aged woman dressed in a scarlet designer dress that fitted her model-svelte figure like a glove.

'To think that when you invited Harry and me here tonight I had no idea that your guest of honour was going to be my dear Petra's daughter. And such a clever and beautiful daughter. Petra would have been so proud of you, Lily. Proud of you and happy for you,' she emphasised, giving Marco a meaningful look before turning back to Lily. 'Emotional happiness was always so important to your mother. I could never understand what she meant about the importance of love until I met my Harry.'

Smiling at the Duchess, she told her friend, 'Carolina, this is such a wonderful coincidence. Lily's mother was one of my closest friends. We modelled together.' She gave a small sigh. 'A lifetime ago now. Petra was younger than me, and such a lovely girl.'

Melanie turned back to Lily, still holding her hands. 'Lily, you are the image of her. I remember when you were born. Your father was still furious with your mother for having a baby. He didn't even go to see her when she was in hospital—just as though he had nothing at all to do with your arrival into the world. He bullied her dreadfully to lose weight, of course, so that she could go back to modelling.'

'Your mother was a model?' Marco demanded, his mistrust and suspicion returning along with his angry contempt. If Lily's mother had been a model that meant she would have even more cause to know just what could happen to the unwary—and yet she had still tried to inveigle his nephew into it. The loathing he felt for the kind of people who had brought about Olivia's destruction surged through Marco's veins.

'Not just a model, but *the* model of her time— just as Lily's father was the photographer of his generation. I'm not surprised to hear from Carolina that you use photography in your own work, Lily. I can still remember watching you playing in your father's studio as a little girl. Even then you preferred taking photographs rather than being in them. Your father was a genius with the camera and a wonderful success in the fashion world.' She looked at Marco. 'Given your relationship with Lily, though, I'm sure that she will have told you that whilst her father was brilliantly successful as a photographer he was a disastrous husband and father. I understand his second marriage broke up as well, Lily?'

Melanie had obviously taken Marco's fixed concentration on what she was saying as a sign that he wanted to hear more, Lily decided miserably. Because without waiting for Lily to answer she continued, 'I can remember going into the studio and seeing Lily playing there on the floor. You were such a sweet-natured, pretty child, Lily, and you could have been the perfect child model. No wonder Anton wanted all those pictures of you.'

Champagne nearly spilled from Lily's glass as she made a sudden rejecting movement she couldn't control. Her hand was trembling uncontrollably, her stomach heaving with sick dread, and she looked towards the door, desperate to escape.

Something was wrong. Something was *very* wrong, Marco was forced to recognise, and the rebellion within him rose up and totally overwhelmed the weakened force of his determination to remain distant from Lily. It was that rebellion and not he himself that had him moving towards her, putting himself between her and the others to shield her, taking hold of her arm to steady her, taking charge and obliterating any resistance. Lily looked numbly at him, like a hunted, tormented creature in fear for its life, caught in a car's headlights.

'Anton liked photographing her, then, did he?' the rebellion in him asked conversationally, mercilessly silencing what he thought of as his real self when it tried to protest that it didn't want to get involved.

'Oh, yes,' Melanie agreed. 'He always said she had real model potential…'

Lily struggled to subdue the sound of protest and anguish rising in her throat. She looked ill,

Marco recognised. Bruised and defeated and agonised.

'I was so sorry when I heard about your mother's death, Lily,' Melanie added in a much more sombre voice. 'Such a dreadfully sad thing to happen.'

'She was never able to come to terms with her divorce from my father,' Lily responded in a strained voice, somehow managing to drag herself back from the edge of the dark, greedy chasm of fear that had opened up at her feet.

The other woman patted her arm and then excused herself, explaining, 'I must go—my husband will be looking for me. Stay in touch, Lily darling.'

The Duchess too had moved away to talk to another guest, leaving Lily alone with Marco in their own little pool of silence.

Marco was still looking at her, even though he had now released her arm, and Lily could imagine what he was thinking. Draining her glass, she turned to him and spoke in an empty voice.

'My mother committed suicide—drink and

prescription drugs. Oh, yes,' she added fiercely when he didn't speak, 'I *do* know what the modelling business can do to those who are too vulnerable for its cruelty. I've experienced it at first hand. That's why...'

Without waiting to see what his response was she stepped past him and walked away, her head held high and half blinded by the tears she knew she dared not shed. She didn't stop in her headlong flight until she realised that she'd lost her way and was in a small ante-room, thankfully all on her own. She wanted fresh air—fresh air and privacy—and the self-indulgence of crying for a mother and a childhood that were long gone. But she wasn't here to indulge herself, she reminded herself sharply. She was here to work. But the floodgates had been opened and there was no holding back the memories now.

CHAPTER EIGHT

SHE knew who the hands on her shoulders belonged to without needing to turn round.

Marco. It couldn't be anyone else.

And the reason she knew was because…because she would know him anywhere. Because with her emotions exposed to the painful air of recognition by Melanie's revelations she had committed the worst self-injury of all. Because there were no other hands she wanted to hold her, only his.

When had her emotions become entangled with her desire for him? When had they melded together to create the most eternally binding human cord of all? Love. Ah, how the mere thought of it threatened pain. She couldn't love Marco. He was turning her round and wrapping his arms around her, holding her as carefully as though she might break. Out of pity, she told herself fiercely. Out of pity—nothing else. And pity wasn't what she wanted from him. She knew that now. She tried to break free but he wouldn't let her go

'You're right,' she told him, as though he had made the statement. 'I'm here to work, not to behave like a silly fool who can't control her emotions.'

The rebellion that had begun as a small pro-test he could easily control had become a raging force for change within him, directing him into responses that should have felt awkward and unwelcome but which instead seemed to come fatally easily. It seemed the most natural thing in the world for him to demand, in a voice that was low and rough with something that could have been self-condemnation, 'Why didn't you tell me any of this before.'

'Tell you what? Tell you that my father was a photographer? Tell you that my mother was a model? Tell you that between them the world of modelling and my father destroyed her, and that

because of that I've…?' Lily's voice thinned out
to become brittle and self-derisory. 'Why should
you want to know? Why should you or anyone
else care?'

Marco could hear the pain she was trying to
control. It seared through him, burning through
the restraints he had wrapped around his own
emotions. An answering pain mixed with yearning and an entirely male desire to hold and protect
her spilled over. To say what he had felt listening
to Melanie's revelations had been shock didn't
come anywhere near describing the effect those
revelations had had on him. They had pierced the
seal he had placed on his own emotions, exposing them to the raw reality of another person's
pain. Lily's pain.

Now he felt as though he was at war with himself—with one part of him wanting to comfort
her and the other defensively wanting him to
ignore what had happened, desperately wanting
him to ignore the voice inside him that was telling him that he and Lily shared a unique bond
forged in pain. Deep within himself emotions he

couldn't afford to let himself feel were struggling to find a voice. The scar tissue he had forced to grow over them was being ripped from old wounds, and against the pressure of his denial the words came out.

'I once knew a girl who became a model.'

His harsh and reluctant admission caused Lily to look at him in surprise. Something in the way he had spoken as much as the words themselves jerked her out of her own distress to register his need. She lifted her hand, as though she was going to reach out and touch him, and then let it drop again, saying uncertainly, 'She was important to you?'

'Yes.' Another admission was wrenched from him; another clamp removed from the resolve-clad box in which he had locked away his right to feel emotional pain. 'We were to have been married.'

Married? Marco had been going to *marry* someone?

'She's dead now. That sordid world killed her.'

Sometimes there were things that were too

painful to know, Lily acknowledged, and this was one of them. She was still in Marco's arms, but now she felt she had no right to be there and that the sanctuary they provided rightly belonged to someone else.

'I'm so sorry.' She tried to step back from him, but instead of releasing her his hold on her tightened. He was so lost in his pain that he was barely aware he was holding her, Lily suspected.

'I couldn't protect her and she died. I tried, but I failed.' Now that the seal damming his past had been pierced the feelings he had locked away for so long flooded past his defences, leaving him powerless to stop himself from revealing the self-contempt he had always tried to keep hidden.

'We grew up together. A marriage between us was what our families had always hoped for. It seemed the right thing to do. We got on well together. She understood the demands of my position. I thought that she knew me and I knew her. I believed I could trust her with anything—my hopes, my doubts, our future together. I believed she trusted me, but I was wrong.'

'I'm sorry,' Lily repeated

'She'd always told me she was happy with our parents' plans for our shared future. I didn't know that she wasn't. She lied to me.'

'Perhaps she didn't want to hurt you and was trying to protect you?' Lily suggested gently, wanting to ease his pain.

Marco looked at her.

At no time had anyone—not Olivia and not even himself—suggested that Olivia might have wanted to spare him pain. Lily's words, her gentleness and her concern for him, felt like the comforting and healing effect of warm sunlight on an unbearably dark, cold place. But he was giving in to something he must not give in to. He was letting the dangerous sweetness that Lily had brought him overwhelm reality. There were still anomalies in Lily's way of life that logic insisted did not add up

'We'd better get back to the reception. The Duchess will be wondering where we are,' Lily warned him.

'In a minute. First I want you to explain to

me what you were doing working in that photographic studio, given what Melanie said about your childhood. I would have thought that it would be the last place you'd want to be after what. I've now learned about you.'

'I was standing in for my half-brother,' Lily admitted. Now he knew about her parents she felt strong enough to tell him the truth, and then at last he would believe her. 'My father married a second time. My stepmother was very kind to me. She's remarried now—my father died ten years ago—but my half-brother has turned our father into a hero figure and wants to follow in his footsteps.'

She gave a small sigh. 'He texted me asking me to stand in for him because he knew I was in Milan. I hadn't realised then that he'd asked your nephew to model for him.'

She was telling him the truth, Marco recognised on an unsettling surge of uncomfortable guilt. 'Why didn't you tell me any of that before?'

'I didn't think you'd believe me,' Lily told him wryly.

'I probably wasn't ready to listen even if you had. I'm sorry I misjudged you. '

'Something like that,' Lily agreed. It was impossible for her to tell him now that she had wanted to keep a distance between them because she had feared the effect he had on her. After all, now she not only knew that he did not reciprocate the desire she felt for him, she also knew he was still mourning the girl he had expected to marry.

She started to walk towards the door, conscious of her duty to the Duchess and her work, but came to an abrupt halt when Marco caught up with her and asked, 'And Anton? Tell me about him?'

Lily's breath escaped in a soft hiss of anxiety. 'There's nothing to tell.'

She was lying, Marco knew, but instead of feeling the sense of condemnation against her he would normally have felt instead he felt an unfamiliar stirring of—of what? Curiosity? Or was it something more personal than that? Something that was in fact concern for her?

Whilst he battled with his own thoughts Lily continued walking back to the reception. She looked so vulnerable and so determined to be strong. No one should have to find strength on their own, without someone who cared about them to help them. He knew the desolate wilderness that place was. He couldn't let Lily struggle in it. He strode after her, catching up with her to put his hand under her elbow so that they re-entered the reception together.

Lily didn't know whether to feel relieved or embarrassed when she realised that the Duchess had put their disappearance down to a desire to be alone with one another. Of course it was true that the presence of Marco's arm around her was hardly likely to convince the Duchess that she had got things wrong, but somehow Lily found it foolishly impossible to move away from his pseudo-lover-like hold.

The rest of the evening passed in something of a tired blur for Lily after the emotional trauma of the day. Of course she managed to stop dwelling on her own feelings when the Duchess showed her and Marco over the long gallery housing the villa's art collection, her professionalism cutting in whilst she made notes and took photographs.

'No wonder you're so professional—you must have been handling these things practically from your cradle,' Marco commented at one point, picking up her camera.

'Practically,' Lily agreed. 'Not that I ever had much of an interest in fashion. It was always art that fascinated me.'

'Not modern art, though?'

'The past feels more comfortable, more established. I feel safer there,' Lily told him, only realising when she saw the way he was looking at her just what she might have betrayed.

'Safer?'

'With art of the past there's no need for me to trust my own judgement,' she defended herself.

'Safety and your desire for it seems to be a recurring theme in your life.'

Lily could feel her heart hammering heavily into her ribs.

'The price of having parents who quarrelled a lot and being over-sensitive to that quarrelling, I expect.'

She was glad that the Duchess was there, to keep the conversation from getting too personal, glad too of the other guests who'd been invited to join them for dinner, so that conversation around the dinner table was kept general.

Inevitably, though, the evening came to an end, and she smiled a goodnight at the Duchess before walking up the stairs and then along the corridor with Marco to the guest suite.

'You can use the bathroom first if you wish,' she said, as soon as they were inside the sitting room. 'I've got some notes I want to type up, so I'll be working for a while.'

Marco nodded his head.

He wasn't anywhere near as immune to her as he should be—as he wanted to be, as he must be. Just because she had shown sympathy toward him over Olivia that did not mean... It didn't mean what? That she wanted him? He could *make* her want him. They both had a shared history of pain, and a shared need to have that pain assuaged. He could assuage it. He could hold her and take her and show her that there was far more pleasure to be found in his arms than in the arms of a man she feared as well as desired.

What was he thinking? All the old habits and teaching rose up inside him, warning him against allowing her to get under his guard. They might have some common ground, but that did not mean that he could trust her.

'I'll say goodnight, then,' he told her curtly, opening the communicating door between the two rooms.

'Yes. Yes. Goodnight,' Lily returned.

It was true that she had work to do, Lily reminded herself, smothering a yawn after the door had closed, leaving her alone in the sitting room to their suite. She sat down at the small pretty desk and opened her laptop, connecting her camera to it so that she could download the photographs she had taken.

Normally within seconds of starting on a task

like this she would have been so absorbed in her work that she'd have been oblivious to anything and everything else, but tonight for some reason, even though she was focusing on the photographs she had taken, her real attention was on the mental images stored inside her head—images of Marco from earlier in the evening. Marco smiling at her as the Duchess introduced them as a couple. Marco steadying her arm when shock had jolted through her, Marco telling her about the love he had lost.

Lily rubbed her eyes and got up, walking up and down and trying to clear her head. Her eyes felt gritty and dry. Her head was beginning to ache. She was tired, but she dared not risk going through the bedroom to the bathroom to get ready for bed until she was sure that Marco was asleep. Perhaps she could just lie down on the sofa for a few minutes…

Marco looked at his watch. Was Lily still working? It was over an hour since he'd come to bed, and she'd looked tired when they'd come upstairs. It was concern for the efficient execution of the tour that was getting him out of bed now, not his concern for Lily herself, he assured himself as he pulled on a bathrobe and opened the communicating door.

Lily's laptop was still open on the desk, quietly humming, but Lily herself had fallen asleep on the sofa, fully dressed.

Why hadn't she made herself properly comfortable? He told himself that what her obvious discomfort was arousing in him was merely irritation. Why should he be concerned for her, after all? He switched off the laptop, intending to walk away and leave her where she was, but something beyond his control made him go back to look down at her a second time. She couldn't possibly sleep properly where she was. At the very least she'd probably wake up with a stiff neck, and that was bound to effect her ability to work—which was why she was here. Sofas and chairs were not designed to be slept on, especially elegant antique pieces—as he knew to his cost.

Conversely, the bed in the bedroom was vast, with plenty of room for two people to sleep in it without having to go anywhere near one another. It seemed ungentlemanly to leave her where she was, as though doing so broke his own expectation of courtesy for someone who was, after all, in his care.

He reached down to wake her up, and then stopped. She would only argue with him and insist on staying where she was, insist that he had the right to the bed. It would be far more expedient to simply pick her up and carry her to the bed than to get involved in an argument in which they'd both fight to be the one to do the right thing.

When he lifted her in his arms she made a small sound that had him catching his breath thinking she was going to wake up, but she merely turned into his body. The sensation of her warmth lying against him sent his heart hammering into his ribs. What was the matter with him? He wasn't so unable to control his needs that he was now afraid of even this kind of intimacy with her, was he?

He felt Lily snuggle deeper into his hold, exhaling a small sigh of pleasure as she did so. Pulling back the covers, Marco placed her down on one side of the bed, and then removed his robe so that he could get into the opposite side of the bed and switch off the bedside lamp. He saw Lily frown in her sleep and move, seeking the warmth that she'd lost. Marco lay on his own side of the bed, his muscles coiled tightly with tension as he willed Lily not to breach the distance he had put between them.

But no amount of willing Lily to stay where she was on his part had the power to come between Lily herself and the need that sleep and his touch had awakened in her. She moved towards him, sighing softly when she found him, curling up against him with her hand on his arm, her head on his chest. He wanted to push her away, but somehow he couldn't. Somehow that rebellion inside him was overriding the instinct that told him that allowing such intimacy between them was dangerous.

He had never slept with a woman so intimately—never allowed himself to gather anyone into his arms and simply hold them. He had never wanted to—until now. Such intense intimacy was not something he felt comfortable with. His parents had lived with a great deal of formality. They had always had separate bedrooms. But right now holding Lily so close to him was exactly what he wanted. He drew her closer and felt the tightening of an unfamiliar ache around his heart. Now he knew why he had always rejected this kind of intimacy. He had rejected it because it was dangerous. Because it made you vulnerable to the woman you were holding. Because once you had known it you would never want to be without it—or without her.

Soft morning light filtered in through the room's curtains, caressing the faces of the two people sleeping together in the centre in the large bed. Lily was held within the protective curve of Marco's body, his arm round her. She was oblivious to the intimacy she had sought—and found—during the night hours whilst she had slept.

Marco woke first, his senses enjoying the knowledge that he was holding Lily before he was properly awake and his brain kicked in to tell him what that meant. When it did, though, he still didn't release her or move away from her. He was trying to work out exactly what it was about holding her that made the intimacy seem not just right but also necessary, he told himself, defending his reluctance to put any distance between them.

She looked so beautiful. She *was* beautiful—inside and out. She was everything any man could ever want in a woman, and the man who had let her go was a fool to have done so. Marco's heart slammed into his ribs, and the small involuntary movement he made, as though in denial of his own thoughts and the reality of what they meant, woke Lily from her sleep.

If she kept her eyes closed perhaps she wouldn't

have to wake up, and then she could hold on to her wonderful dream of being held safe in Marco's arms. Mmm… In her imagination she was there still, and she could feel his heart beating against the hand she had placed on his bare chest. She *could* feel his heart beating beneath her hand. Lily's eyes flew open. She was in bed with Marco and he was holding her. How had that happened? Had she somehow sleep-walked into the bedroom and got into bed beside him? She hoped not.

She looked at Marco, who immediately released her and removed himself from the bed, reaching for his robe as he did so, telling her with a dismissive shrug, 'You didn't look very comfortable sleeping on the sofa, so I brought you here. I thought there was more than enough room in the bed for both of us.' His voice was terse, his manner distant. He disappeared into the bathroom before she could say anything.

Thankfully, Lily realised she was still fully dressed. She was uncomfortably aware that she must have been the one to initiate their sleeping intimacy, given the way she had been dreaming about him. Why hadn't he demanded an explanation of her behaviour? Perhaps because he was so used to sleeping with eager women—women he couldn't love because he loved a girl who was now lost to him for ever—who longed to be close to him that what she had done had barely registered with him.

Lily's heart felt very heavy indeed.

They'd had a very busy full day, visiting two more villas in the morning and stopping briefly for a light lunch before continuing on to visit a private villa on one of Lake Como's small islands. Yet no amount of busyness was enough to push out of her thoughts everything that she'd felt on waking up in Marco's arms this morning. It was like holding a special golden treasure whose existence was enough to fill her with happiness. Her treasure, though, was fool's gold—because it meant nothing to Marco. *She* meant nothing to Marco.

It was now late in the afternoon, and they had

stopped in a pretty lakeside town for a cup of coffee at Marco's suggestion, prior to their return to the villa.

Marco had just gone inside the café to pay their bill, and she was sitting drinking in the relaxing scene around her, when to her horrified disbelief she saw Anton Gillman on the other side of the road. She had assumed and hoped that he had left the area, with the rest of the fashion pack and returned to Milan, but obviously she had been wrong. Lily shrank back in her chair, hoping that he wouldn't look across the road and see her. For a moment she thought that he wouldn't, and that she was safe, but then the woman seated at a table close to their own got up, her small lap dog barking shrilly. The sound caught Anton's attention so that he glanced towards the café. There was nowhere for her to hide, no hope that he wouldn't see her, and Lily knew that he had when she saw him start to cross the road and come purposefully towards her. It was the worst kind of cruel coincidence.

Lily shuddered to see the admiring looks he

was attracting from the woman with the yapping dog. She was quite obviously impressed by his air of authority, his expensive suit and his immaculate grooming. If only she knew the truth about him and his sexual tastes she wouldn't be so interested in him or so admiring.

Lily wasn't impressed, though. She was a teenage girl again, sick with fear and loathing because she knew what he wanted from her.

He was smiling at her—that taunting, cruel smile she had never been able to forget.

'Lily, my lovely.' His voice caressed her as his knuckles stroked along her jaw, and his gaze registered her immediate terrified recoil from him. 'Delicious that you've remained so...sensitive. I shall enjoy discovering just how sensitive when I finally persuade you to give in to me.'

Inside the café, waiting to pay their bill, Marco saw the tall dark-haired man approaching Lily and recognised him immediately. Her ex-lover. Anger and jealousy surged over him. There were two people ahead of him in the queue to pay, one of them an elderly man who obviously couldn't see very well, and who was struggling to find the right money. Marco saw the man lean towards Lily, who was out of view. The intensity of the emotion that exploded inside him scorched the truth of his feelings into him. He was jealous. He was jealous of another man's right to claim Lily's attention and to claim Lily herself because… Because she meant far more to him than he had previously allowed himself to admit?

The elderly man was still fumbling with his money, and the woman behind him in the queue was tutting in her impatience, but Marco was oblivious to them both. How had it happened? How could it be that Lily had become so important to him? He didn't know. He only knew that she was—just as he knew that this was the last thing he had ever have wanted to happen. He had built a life that depended on him not becoming emotionally involved with others, on not allowing himself to become emotionally dependent on anyone. How had Lily managed to slip beneath his guard and touch that place within him where he was so dangerously vulnerable? His formidable inner defences were warning him to step back from the danger that now lay ahead of him, to turn round and walk away from it—and from Lily herself.

It was illogical for her to feel so afraid, Lily tried to reassure herself. Anton couldn't do anything to harm her now. She was an adult, not a teenager, and they were in public. She was in command of her own life. But some fears could not be controlled with mere reason, and this one had lived privately hidden within her for a very long time.

'Why don't we take a little walk, you and I?' Anton suggested. 'I'm sure your companion won't mind, *Dr* Wrightington.'

Lily's stomach swooped sickeningly. He'd been checking up on her, asking questions about her.

'I'm not going anywhere with you.'

Too late she recognised it was the wrong thing to say, with its echoes of past refusal.

Where was Marco? Why hadn't he come back? What if he didn't come back?

She looked frantically into the café willing Marco to see her and come to her rescue, but she couldn't see him because of the customers blocking her view. She was alone with Anton. Abandoned by Marco just as she had been abandoned by her father. There was no one to support her, no one to protect her.

Hadn't it always been that way? Hadn't she always had to protect herself? Hadn't she always been alone and uncared for by those she'd longed so much to love her? Her mother, her father, Marco… She was so afraid, so alone. She had to get away, to escape. She stood up, her abrupt movement causing her chair to scrape on the stone beneath it with an ugly grating sound, and her panic increased when Anton took advantage of her fear to take hold of her arm.

In the shop the elderly man had finally paid his bill, scooping up his change with quivering hands, and now the woman was handing over her money.

Marco looked towards the table where he had left Lily. She was standing up now, the man with her taking her arm. They were standing close together. Had Lily forgotten that the man holding her, the man she was about to give herself to, had already let her down once? If so, then perhaps he should remind her. And risk being told that he was interfering where his interference wasn't wanted, as it had been with Olivia? Risk being accused of trying to ruin her life?

In his mind's eye Marco could see his eighteen-year-old self, humiliated and shamed. He would not be endure that kind of humiliation again.

Turning his back on the scene being played out beyond the interior of the café, Marco continued to wait to pay their bill.

'Ah, poor Lily—still so afraid of me. How delicious and erotic…even more so now than when you were younger. There is nothing quite like a little bit of fear to add spice to…things.'

Something snapped inside Lily. Instinct and need pushed aside the rules of modern-day life that told her it was her duty to herself and others not to make a nuisance of herself, not to ask anything of anyone, not to expect others to help her or to forge an emotional bond with her that meant she could turn to them in need. In a last despairing surge she turned towards the interior of the café. She could see Marco now. He was paying their bill.

'*Marco...*'

The anguished, almost sobbed sound of Lily's voice calling his name drew Marco's gaze in her direction. She was looking at him—looking for him. Her free arm—the arm her companion was not holding—was stretched out toward him. She needed him. Lily *needed* him!

Throwing down a note over twice the value of the coffees they had just had, Marco ran towards the door.

Lily exhaled in relief. Marco had heard her. He was going to help her.

He reached her, grasping her free hand, holding it safe.

'Make him go away, Marco,' she begged him

wildly, unable to control her distress. 'Please make him go away.'

'You heard Lily,' Marco told Anton, confronting her persecutor and impaling him with a coldly hostile look of warning.

Anton didn't move, saying mockingly instead, 'Naughty Lily. You never told me that you have a new...protector.'

Whilst Lily flinched Marco didn't shift his concentration from the other man's face. No matter what the relationship between Lily and this man might have been before, it was to *him* that she was now appealing for rescue and refuge, and Marco's nature and upbringing would not allow him to deny her either.

'Any decent man would consider it his duty to protect a woman from your sort,' Marco told Anton curtly. 'And let me warn you that my protection of Lily will extend beyond this incident. You would be well advised to keep away from her in future. In fact, I'd advise you to leave Italy today."

The smirking self-confidence with which

Anton had greeted Marco's arrival had evap-
orated now into blustering protest as he complained, 'You can't make that kind of threat.'

'I'm not threatening you,' Marco assured him.
'I'm simply giving you some advice as a result
of your own behaviour.'

Lily listened to their exchange with gratitude
and awe. Marco was being magnificent. He
was so completely in control, so completely the
master of the situation, completely demolishing
Anton who, having released her when Marco arrived on the scene, was now backing off, eventually turning his back on them to disappear into
the crowd. She looked at Marco. He was standing
rather stiffly to one side of her, looking away
from her.

Marco knew something had happened to him.
Something that threatened his defences. His
throat felt raw and tight—with tension, nothing
else, he assured himself. He looked back at Lily.
She looked stricken, but she didn't say anything.
Her face was paper-white as she turned away
from him, dignified in defeat, her manner that

of a weary combatant struggling to pick up her weapons and continue to fight on alone. She looked alone. He knew all about how that felt— how it hurt, how the heart hardened around that hurt.

She was trembling violently, her manner that of someone too traumatised to be able to behave rationally. Whatever had happened between her and her ex whilst Marco had been paying their bill had plainly affected her very badly. He stepped towards her, and then checked himself and stepped back. He wanted to cross the chasm that separated him from obeying his instincts but years of denying those instincts, had laid down rules inside him that had to be obeyed. The voices of his inner rebellion were growing stronger, urging him to join them, but he couldn't. Because he was too afraid. Afraid of being deceived and betrayed. Out of nowhere, out of nothing he could understand, something inside him rejected that possibility, stating clearly and firmly that Lily wouldn't do that to him.

All around them people were going about their

business, but for Marco his world had come to a halt and was now poised trembling on the brink of something momentous. *Lily.* His heart pounded and surged inside his chest cavity, as though trying to break free of unwanted bonds. Lily. She had turned to him. She had wanted his help and she had trusted him to give it. Trust. Trust was a rare and precious gift when it was exchanged between two people. Lily had offered him the gift of her trust, and that gift demanded surely that he reciprocate in kind. Trust Lily? Trust anyone with his own vulnerabilities? He couldn't. He scarcely trusted himself with them. That was why he had had to lock them away.

A car horn sounded in the traffic and the moment was gone, banished by the demands of the real world. The danger had passed. The path he had laid down for himself had forked, and briefly he had been tempted to take the wrong fork, but thankfully he had recognised the folly of doing so. Practicality reasserted itself within him, much to his relief—if for no other reason than because it was easier to deal with practical matters than it was for him to deal with emotions.

They had finished their work for the day and, whilst he'd intended to take Lily on a tour of a silk mill as she'd requested, it was plain to Marco that right now she was in no state to do anything. The best thing he could do was get her back to the privacy of the Duchess's villa.

She didn't speak as they were driven back to the villa, simply sat stiffly at his side, her stiffness occasionally broken by the tremors that shook her body.

The Duchess was out visiting friends, and Lily made no objection when Marco suggested that she might want to rest in their room, letting him guide her up the stairs and along the corridor to their suite, where she subsided onto the bed, sitting tensely at its edge as she spoke for the first time. 'Please don't leave me here on my own,' she begged.

'You're safe now, Lily,' Marco responded. 'He can't come back into your life now—unless you choose to ask him to do so.'

'Ask Anton into my life?' Lily shuddered. 'Never. *Never...*'

'You must have cared for him once.' The cool words, a product of his suspicion and refusal to trust, were forced into the open by those voices within him that warned he had already let down his guard far too much, and that now was the time to rectify that mistake whilst he still could.

But they made Lily flinch visibly, causing him to feel an unexpected stab of guilt as she denied emotionally, 'No. Never. I disliked him from the start. But he was my father's friend and I couldn't avoid him.'

She had met the other man through her *father*? Even the logical, searching, suspicious voice within him had to accept that that changed things—but it still insisted on reminding her, 'You were lovers.'

CHAPTER NINE

LILY raised her head and looked up at Marco, revulsion darkening her eyes. Marco's words had filled her with anguish and fear, flooded her mind with memories that undermined her already shaky self-control.

She had kept her secrets to herself for so long—refusing to unburden herself to anyone, bearing the horror of them alone—but now suddenly everything was too much for her. She couldn't go on any longer. She couldn't bear the pain and the guilt any more.

She was shivering and trembling, lost in the grip of her emotions and the past.

'No!' she told Marco vehemently. 'No. I would never let him even touch me.' She shuddered. 'I hated him—loathed him.' The words gathered speed, spilling out of her in jerky uncoordinated sentences. 'He kept saying things to me…looking at me…even though he knew how much I hated him. That just made him laugh. He said that he'd get his way in the end and that I wouldn't be able to stop him. I told him I'd tell my father, but he just laughed at me. I was only fourteen, and my father…'

She shuddered again and Marco listened, every word she uttered a fresh lash of anguished guilt against new emotions still raw from having the protective cover he had used to smother them ripped from them. Whilst he had been clinging to his refusal to trust her she had been at the mercy of her tormentor.

Like a river dammed from its original course and now returning to it, feelings, emotions and awareness were starting to flow back over dry, parched land that was now struggling to cope with the flood, whilst the other course fought desperately to hold on to its supremacy. As always when his emotions seemed to threaten him, Marco took refuge in practical action, going to the cabinet in the sitting room and opening it, pouring Lily a small glass of brandy which he took back to her, instructing her, 'Drink this.' When she hesitated, he assured her, 'You're in shock and it will help you.'

Nodding her head, Lily tilted the glass to her lips. The fiery liquid burned its way down her throat, warming her stomach, leaving her feeling slightly light-headed.

Why had she told Marco what she had? She wished desperately that she hadn't, but it was too late to deny her admission now. She stood up abruptly, ignoring the dizzy feeling that instantly seized her as she paced the floor at the end of the bed, lost, trapped in a world of fear and despair.

Marco felt the full weight of the enormity of what she had said to him. She was carrying a terrible burden of emotional pain. He could see that now. A burden of pain *he* had reinforced by his cruel misjudgement of her. Like a blind man trying to seek his way in unfamiliar territory he tried to understand what he should do—for her, not for himself, because it was her need that mattered to him now. Comforting her was far more important to him than protecting his own emotional distance. He wanted to help her, he recognised. He wanted to comfort her, wanted to love her. *Love* her? He wanted to *love* her.

Quickly he pushed the admission away. There were things that Lily needed to say. Things she had kept locked away inside herself for a very long time, and he knew all about the darkness that could cause.

'Tell me what happened, Lily,' he urged her gently. 'Tell me about him…Anton.'

Lily looked at him, as though properly registering his presence for the first time. 'I can't,' she answered him. 'You wouldn't understand. You think I'm a liar.'

Her words struck like a blow against his conscience.

'I *will* understand and I *will* believe you,' he promised her, adding quietly, 'You said it was your father who introduced you to him?'

'Yes. Anton owns one of the magazines that used to commission my father. He used to come to my father's studio.'

'And that was where you met him?'

'Yes. I didn't like him right from the start. There was something about him.' Lily closed her eyes, but she couldn't blot out the memories and the images she didn't want to see. 'He knew that I didn't like him. I could tell. It amused him. He enjoyed...he liked frightening me. And I *was* afraid of him. He made me afraid of him. Just by looking at me sometimes. I used to have nightmares about him looking at me.'

Marco swallowed down on the angry pity her words had produced.

'What about your parents? Your mother...?'

'My mother was dead by then, and my stepmother had left my father, taking Rick with her. I was at boarding school, so most of the time I was...I didn't have to see him. It was just during the school holidays, when I was staying with my father.'

'Didn't you tell him how you felt?'

'I couldn't. He wouldn't have understood. My father... Well, you heard Melanie. He never really wanted children.'

Maybe not, but having had them surely he must have accepted that it was his duty as a father to protect his child? Marco thought grimly, but he didn't want to upset Lily even more by saying so.

As though she sensed what he was thinking, and his criticism of her father, she told him quickly, 'They were friends—and not just that. My father worked for Anton. As you know, my father was a photographer. He worked for several upmarket magazines, doing modelling shoots. He and the people he mixed with were very cutting edge. They lived a certain kind of lifestyle. I suppose the best way to sum it up is to say that it was a…a sex, drugs and rock and roll lifestyle.'

'And Anton also lived that lifestyle?'

'Yes. He was—still is, I suppose—a very wealthy man. A very important man in the fashion world. His magazine is hugely influential. Being commissioned to photograph fashion shoots for it was an accolade. It could make or break a photographer. My father lived for his work. It gave him the kind of high that other people get from drugs. He was very creative, a genius in his field, and he would get angry and impatient with people who got in the way of him fulfilling his talent.'

'Meaning that he didn't have much time for those close to him?' Marco guessed.

'My stepmother was better at dealing with him than my mother, but even she lost patience with him in the end. Rick, my half-brother, worships the memory of our father and wants to follow in his footsteps—but of course he never really knew him properly.'

'Unlike you. So, Anton and your father were friends?'

'Yes. I remember the summer I was fourteen he seemed to be at the studio all the time. When Dad wasn't there he'd ask to take some...some nude shots of me, and I refused. I remember Dad being furious with me when I tried to tell him.'

'Why? What did he say?'

'He refused to believe me—accused me of attention-seeking. Being just like my mother. It was a horrible holiday. Dad refused to speak to me, and then just before I went back to school my stepmother told me that she was divorcing him. I liked her. I still do. She was kind to me— that's why I feel I owe it to her to keep an eye on Rick, as well, of course, as because he's my half-brother. She's remarried now, and she lives in California. She's always inviting me out to stay but I haven't managed it as yet.

'Rick always says that it isn't fair that Dad taught me to use a camera but died before he could teach him. I couldn't have *not* learned, really. Well, I couldn't have had him for a father and not learned how to take a photograph. I always preferred to photograph things, though, not people. It felt safer, somehow. The camera catches things that the naked eye doesn't always, you see. My mother…. Well, in some of the last photographs of her I think you can see how desperate she was, how alone she felt. I wish I'd been able to help her.

'Anyway, after that whenever I came home from school for the holidays Anton always

seemed to be there, at the studio, and I noticed...'
She paused.

This was so difficult.

'You noticed?' Marco repeated, his voice so devoid of emotion that its calmness steadied her.

She still couldn't look at him, though, so she went to stand in front of the window as she told him in a low voice, 'I noticed that the models my father was being asked to photograph for Anton's magazine were getting younger and younger. That wasn't entirely unusual for the time. The modelling world was changing, and the demand was for younger girls. But Anton's magazine seemed to use more of them than anyone else. There was one girl—Anna. She was so pretty, so very pretty, and young—only fifteen. I really liked her. She wasn't like the other models. She was still at school, like me, but I was at boarding school in the country and she was at a London day-school. Her mother was a dancer and her parents were divorced too. Her father didn't ap-prove of her modelling. She told me that her agent said she thought she'd be doing a *Vogue* cover by the end of the year, only she didn't.'

Her voice became suspended. 'I'm sorry. I can't… It was so awful, so horrible.'

'What happened, Lily?'

Marco suspected he knew what she was going to say, and he was appalled.

'It's the reason I still hate going in helicopters—because we travelled to the shoot in one that day.' She shuddered at the thought. 'I still feel so guilty because I never said anything,' she told him in a ragged voice, turning round from the window to look at him, her face ravaged by her emotions.

Marco knew all about guilt, and how it ate away at a person. He went to her, wanting to reach out and hold her, but he was held back by his own demons. They told him that if he held her now he would be making a commitment that would bind him to her for ever, and that was a risk he must not take.

He saw Lily's shoulders lift as she breathed in,

taking the kind of breath that someone facing an enormous physical challenge needed to take.

'Anna said that Anton had raped her and she thought she was pregnant. She said that Anton had been coming to the studio to see her, and he'd sent my father away on some pretext so they'd be alone together. She cried when she told me. She said it had been awful and that she was afraid to tell her mother.'

Lily took another deep breath to steady herself.

'That was the day before I was going back to school. I never saw her again. When I asked my father about her he said that Anton had told him she'd stopped modelling because she'd fallen down the stairs to her mother's flat and broken her leg. I wrote to her, but she never wrote back to me. Her mother wrote instead, saying that Anna had gone to live with her father and her stepmother.'

Her voice broke, and Marco could only guess at what she was feeling.

'That was at half-term,' she told him. 'At the start of the Christmas holiday Anton was still always there at the studio.' Her voice grew stronger. 'And then one day, after he and my father had gone out to lunch together, Anton came back but my father didn't.'

Lily swallowed hard.

'It was everything I'd dreaded, but worse. He told me what he wanted to do to me—what he was going to make me do to him.'

Marco's contempt for the other man turned to white-hot rage.

'I told him I'd tell my father, but he just laughed at me. He told me that he had a thing about virgins—young virgins. It was horrible—sickening. I was so afraid that I ran out of the studio. I didn't know what to do or where to go. I had a key to my father's flat, but I was afraid to go there in case somehow he, Anton was there.'

Marco closed his eyes against the anger boiling up inside him—against the man who had wanted to abuse her, against her father, against the whole of his sex for being what it was, but most of all against himself for not recognising her fear and for not protecting her from it.

Marco was so silent, so unmoving. Why didn't he say something? Didn't he know how much she needed comfort from him? How much she needed *him*? Defenceless and drained, Lily could only hold out her arms to him in supplication and beg, 'Hold me, Marco. Please hold me.'

Lily's words shocked through Marco. Hold her? He couldn't. Everything he had taught himself to be recoiled from the thought of such intimacy. He feared the private wounds within himself it might reveal, searing him just as her anguished plea had seared his emotions—those emotions he had fought for so long to deny. If he touched her now he was afraid that he would take her to himself, crush her to himself, and never want to let her go.

Marco was turning away from her—no doubt filled with contempt for her and for her weakness, Lily recognised mutely, and her pent-up breath escaped on a sound that was humiliatingly close to a small sob.

Lily was crying? He had made her cry?

Marco turned round, and from doing that took

a step towards her, ignoring the mental lashing of his brain that urged him to stop. How could he when his heart was aching with remorse and longing?

Lily watched him without speaking, and for a moment Marco thought that she was going to ignore him and walk away from him. Part of him hoped that she would. But then she made a suppressed sound of desperation and almost flung herself against him, wrapping her arms around him, resting her head on his chest, her body trembling against his.

Slowly, awkwardly, uncomfortably, he lifted his own arms and placed them round her. Defeat. Surrender. The giving in of his will to his emotions. It should have felt wrong. *She* should have felt wrong. But instead it felt—she felt… Marco understood as he held her close. It felt as though she completed him. He breathed in and then exhaled slowly and deeply, as though he was releasing a burden he had carried for far too long.

She felt so delicate within his hold, and holding her now, as a woman, Marco could only ache for the fragile, vulnerable girl she must have been. Olivia had never felt like this—but then he had never held her like this. He had never held her at all, really. On those rare occasions when he had kissed her she had never aroused in him a hunger for her, as Lily had done, Marco recognised. Never made him want her and then want equally to reject that wanting because it made him feel vulnerable. Their relationship had been more one of brother and sister than two young people who would one day be husband and wife.

But it was Lily who needed to be the focus of his thoughts now, not Olivia, and most certainly not his own self-centred fear of losing face through his damaged pride.

'And the rest of that Christmas holiday?' he pressed her. 'What happened?'

'I went back to school,' Lily told him, her voice muffled as she kept her face pressed to his shoulder, 'I knew I'd be safe there. There were always some girls there who had to stay at school in the holidays. It was lovely. We had a proper Christmas dinner, and the teachers took us to the theatre and museums. It was like being part of a…a family, and I felt…I knew that I was safe.'

Just as she did now, here with Marco, Lily knew, lifting her head from his shoulder to look at him as she told him, 'I'm so grateful to you for…for being here for me, and for helping me. Thank you.'

She leaned forward, intending to kiss his cheek, but he turned his head in such a swift recoil that her lips brushed his instead, causing him to recoil even further and step back from her.

Mortified, Lily apologised. 'I'm sorry. I didn't intend… I shouldn't have asked you to hold me. It was thoughtless of me when I know that what I told you must have made you think of the girl you were going to marry.'

His response was gruff. 'I was thinking of her, yes.' *But not as much as I was thinking of you,* Marco added to himself privately. *Not as much as I shall be thinking about you for ever.*

It was her own fault if his answer had hurt

her—her own fault because deep inside herself she must have known that she was falling in love with him, Lily castigated herself. She wouldn't have burned for him in the way that she had if it hadn't been for that love. The look on his face made her feel as though her heart was being wrung out and weeping in pain. It was time for her to move on.

'It's been illogical of me to be so afraid of Anton. I'm an adult now, and he can only intimidate me through my fear if I keep that fear,' she told him, trying to make sure her voice sounded purposeful and friendly instead of betraying her aching need for him. 'And what makes that fear even more illogical is that I made sure that I lost my virginity and so removed what it was about me I believed Anton desired the minute I reached my sixteenth birthday.'

Marco bowed his head. He had lost his own virginity at sixteen himself, to an older girl who had seduced him with enthusiasm and what to him at that age had seemed a great deal of expertise, but it had been an emotionless experience.

'It was a goal I'd set myself—a bridge I had to cross and then burn behind me to keep me safe from Anton,' Lily continued. 'As my birthday is in May, it had to be during term-time. At a dance with the boys from a nearby public school a boy asked me to dance who I remembered from the Christmas Dance. I'd liked him because he was quiet and shy. We did the deed with a good deal of fumbling and uncertainty on both sides, more at my instigation than his. It was a practical necessity rather than an…an act of mutual desire, and I have to say that nothing about it has ever made me feel I want to repeat it.'

Marco's heart jolted. It was wrong, so wrong, that all either of them had known of sexual intimacy was a cold, emotionless coming together— even if in the years since his first encounter he had acquired all the necessary physical skills to please his partners. Together they could share something unique, give one another something that neither of them had experienced with anyone else—something that he now knew he would never want to experience with anyone other than her.

Marco considered himself to be a modern man, and indeed something of a pragmatist, but right now, against any kind of logic, there was something inside him that was asking if it *was* merely circumstance that had brought them together.

What was he thinking? That they had been fated to meet? That it had been written into their lives from birth—preordained, in fact? Was that what he wanted to believe? Was that what he wanted to trust, to give himself over to? Just as he yearned for Lily to give herself over to him?

The walls within which he had imprisoned his emotions were crashing down around him and there was no place left for him to hide from them. He must confront them and accept what they were telling him about himself—if he dared.

Lily's hesitant, 'Can I ask you something personal?' had him giving her a wary look before nodding his head.

'Is it just because I was involved in the modelling world that you don't trust me? Or is it because of her…your….your girl as well?' Why was she persisting in adding more pain to the pain she was already enduring? What difference would it make?

None at all. And yet she found herself exhaling unsteadily when Marco agreed brusquely, 'Yes.'

Lily nodded her head, and was about to turn away when Marco added with even more brusque reluctance, 'And it's *didn't*—not don't. I *didn't* trust you—not I don't,' he elucidated, crossing the floor and opening the door, before she could say anything, leaving her to stare after him.

Did he mean that he trusted her now? And if he did… Stop it, Lily warned herself. Stop building impossible hopes out of nothing, because it'll only backfire on you.

CHAPTER TEN

IT WAS over an hour since Marco had left her alone in their suite. An hour in which she had gone over and over their conversation. What had possessed her to say that about there not being anyone since that boy? What had she hoped for?

Did she really need to ask herself that question? She had wanted him to take her back in his arms. She had wanted him to take her to bed and show her—give her, share with her—all the sensual pleasures she knew she would find there with him. She had wanted to give him her love—even if he had no love to give her because he loved someone else.

He loved someone else, but she knew instinctively that, being the man he was—the kind, caring man he sought to hide beneath an outward mask of disdain and arrogance, the man who had rescued her from Anton—were she to ask him, plead with him, beg him to give her what she had never had, his compassion—the compassion she had now discovered ~~the~~ he possessed—would lead to him giving in and giving her what she wanted.

She would do that? She would humiliate herself like that when she knew he loved someone else?

But didn't she have the right to know him as her lover? Didn't she have the right to create memories with him and of him that she could hold long, long after she could no longer hold him? She was on the pill—prescribed by her doctor because of problems she'd been having with her periods—so there was no question of an accidental pregnancy, and something told her that a man like Marco would always place sexual health high on the list of things that were important to him.

She had always sworn not to get sexually involved, in case it led to her falling in love and suffering the pain she had seen her mother go through.

She was already in love with him, though, so that argument no longer held good. She was going to suffer the pain of not being loved by him whether or not they were lovers.

Lovers. Her and Marco. Wasn't that really what she had wanted right from the start?

It was too late now. He had gone. But he would come back, Lily reminded herself, and when he did…

When he did she must think about her pride and do nothing, she warned herself.

Marco hesitated outside the suite door. It was over two hours since he had left Lily to rest, and he wanted to warn her that the Duchess had asked if they would mind dining alone this evening, without her, as she had an engagement she'd overlooked. If Lily preferred she could eat alone in the suite. She was bound to have a reaction to what she'd gone through in telling him about her past, and she might prefer to be alone.

With his admission to Lily that he trusted her the last of his barriers against her had been swept away—kicked away by himself, he acknowledged, because he no longer wanted or needed them. What he needed and wanted was Lily's love, Lily's presence in his life. He had been so wrong about her. Could he bring himself to tell her that? Could he bring himself to let her see his vulnerability and his need? Could he really believe the inner voice that told him he could place his trust in her?

Lily watched as the handle to the suite door turned, her heart lifting and then plummeting downwards in a high dive, the sensation inside her chest echoing the tension of the high-risk strategy she intended to adopt. After all, what had she got to lose?

Her heart? She'd already lost that. Her pride? She didn't care about it. Right now all she cared about was creating enough memories to sustain her through the rest of her life from the handful of hours that were all she would have of Marco. She'd made her plans. If he agreed then later, afterwards—tomorrow morning, in fact—she intended to leave the villa for the airport and

England without completing their tour. That way Marco would be spared the embarrassment and awkwardness of her continued company, and she would be spared having to face the reality of his lack of love for her. Her last memories of him would be those of lying in his arms as his lover.

She didn't think she'd be letting the trust down. She had enough information and commitment already for the exhibition. Of course leaving tomorrow did mean that she'd never get to see Marco's home...

If she did have any regrets they were superficial—a wish that she could have dressed herself for Marco in something more sensually provocative than the bathrobe she was wearing under which she was naked. She hadn't forgotten his reaction to her sensible undies. Better not to wear them than risk putting him off with their practicality and lack of feminine allure.

The door was opening. Her mouth might have gone dry with tension, her heart might be pounding erratically against her ribs, but she was ready.

Ready and oh, so willing and wanting. A small

final mental prayer that things would go well, and then she was positioning herself so that she would be the first thing Marco saw when he walked into the room.

When he did, though, his reaction wasn't what she'd hoped for. She'd somehow envisaged them looking at one another and then her slipping out of her bathrobe and going to him in a shared intense silence. Instead Marco seemed to be avoiding looking at her.

Why hadn't he knocked on the door first? Marco asked himself savagely. If he had he would have saved himself the agony of knowing that Lily was probably naked under that bathrobe, and everything that that knowledge was doing to his self-control. He could almost feel the satin softness of her skin beneath his touch his need for her was so intense. He could almost see her, feel her, taste her, and his body was reacting as though he had. Molten, hot pent-up desire—the kind of desire he had never imagined he could allow himself to feel—was surging through him, taunting him and tormenting him as it swept away his self-control.

He ached for her—and not just physically. His desire for her was passionately emotional. It filled him not just with a need to bind them together in the physical act of love but also with a hunger to bind them together with words as well—the kind of words he had always sworn he would never utter. Words of longing and giving. Words of pleasure and promise. Words that would humbly offer up to her the poor gift of his love and somehow magically win from her the sweet prize of hers.

Words that would give his emotions expression and free them from their imprisonment. The same words that had always been his adversaries, bringing a danger that could rob him of his defences, would now become his aides in the battle to win Lily's heart.

Marco still hadn't moved or spoken, but it wasn't for nothing that Lily had her doctorate. It took her only a handful of seconds to mentally reorganise her plan and see a way of using

Marco's silence as a way of taking charge and setting her own agenda.

She paused to steady her nerves, and then told him, 'I'm so grateful to you, Marco, for helping me to come to terms with…with things, and to leave my past behind and walk freely into my future.'

A future he wanted to share with her, Marco recognised as he listened to her.

'I've got a favour to ask you,' Lily continued.

'If I can help, then you have my word that I will,' Marco responded.

Lily's heart somersaulted. He might not say that when he knew what the favour was.

'I know that you aren't the kind of man who likes to leave a task only partially completed,' she said sedately, 'so I'm hoping…'

Marco waited.

'The thing is…' Lily paused. Did she really have the courage to do this? Thinking about the consequences if she didn't, of all that she would never know or have, was all she needed to convince her that she did.

'Well, the fact of the matter is, Marco, that helping me to get over the effect Anton had on me isn't just about listening to me talking about it. I need your help with something else.'

'Something else?'

Did she want him to pursue Anton and punish him as he deserved for what he had done? He was certainly willing to do so if that was what she wanted.

'I want you to take me to bed and make love to me, please, Marco.'

When she heard the breath he expelled from his lungs, Lily told him quickly, 'I know—I know it's a lot to ask of you. But you are the only person I can ask. You must see that.'

Oh, what a perfidious creature she was—and far more adept at using all the tricks that Eve had given her sex than she had ever imagined.

'If you won't, then how will I ever be able to live a normal life? I've only had sex once, with a boy who was even more nervous about it than I was myself,' she reminded him. 'How can I ever be a proper woman, the woman I really want to be, if I don't even know what it means to be a woman sexually?'

She could see him shaking his head. He was going to refuse.

But instead he said hoarsely, 'You'd trust me to do that…to show you…give you…?'

Lily had never seen him respond so emotionally before, and her heart turned over.

'I trust you completely, Marco. I've never known anyone I could trust more.'

He was looking at her now with something unfathomable and almost tortured in his eyes. Holding her breath, Lily walked towards him, and then, when she was close enough for him to touch her, she let the bathrobe slip to the floor.

'Lily…'

Was the way he said her name a protest or a sign that he was giving in? Lily didn't know, but she did know that she could feel his breath against her lips, and that he wasn't stopping her when she placed her hands on his shoulders and her mouth against his.

'Lily.'

He said her name again. Against her lips this time, taking them beneath his own when they parted, drawing her naked body close to his. She could feel the unmistakable hardness of his arousal and a thrill of relief went through her. It had begun—the journey that would take her from her past to her future, through heartache to a pleasure beyond which lay even more heartache. But she wasn't going to think about that now. For now she was only going to think about Marco, and loving him.

CHAPTER ELEVEN

THEY were on the bed, lying naked there together, and the soft sound of Lily's sighs of pleasure was floating on the air as Marco kissed his way from her shoulder to her ear, causing shimmering showers of lightning pleasure to burst into brilliant life inside her. The touch of his fingertips against her skin as he caressed her provoked a counterpoint sensual response of pleasure, bringing her body to singing, delirious life wherever he touched it. His deliberately slow and careful arousal of her was thrilling it and her with starbursts of erotic delight.

Beneath that pleasure, though, Lily was conscious of a deeper, sharper, keener hunger that had fed on and grown with each small measure of sensual delight until it was beginning to rage fiercely inside her. It was this hunger that she had always feared—this need within her to burn at such an intense heat with love for her lover that her feelings for him could destroy her. The need she had for Marco would never be satisfied by sensual pleasure alone, she knew. It went deeper than that. But for now she would think only of this pleasure and this intimacy, because it was for now that it and Marco would be hers.

Her response to him was magical—a miracle, given what she had endured. Marco struggled to contain and control his own desire for her so that he could concentrate on her experience and her pleasure. He wanted this to be perfect for her. He wanted it to be everything she hoped it to be. He wanted every touch, every sensation she had to show her a fulfilment that would set her completely free from the past.

He cupped her shoulder, stroking her warm, soft skin and then her breast, feeling her shudder and arch her body against his hand, her nipple taut and flushed with desire, her own hands reaching for his shoulders. He kissed the valley between her breasts and then the soft, sweetly fragranced slope, stroking his tongue against her nipple.

Immediately she cried out, her nails digging into his back and her eyes wide with wonder and delight as her breathing accelerated into unsteady swiftness. His own body ached and pulsed, his groin tightening with his need to grind it against her softness in an attempt to reduce the pressure of his desire. But this wasn't about his satisfaction. Not even when he took the hard peak of her nipple into his mouth to suckle it slowly and Lily responded by crying out and gripping his hips, pulling him down against her open thighs. Her actions turned the soft, slow suckle of his mouth on her breast into a fiercely insistent rhythmic demand that came perilously close to making him lose control.

This was what she wanted, Lily acknowledged triumphantly as her body answered the demand of the sexually explicit rhythm Marco was driving into her with the possessive heat of his mouth. Deep within her that same rhythm was pulsing its own growing need, telling her to wrap her legs around him and draw him down against her body.

His need to possess her, to claim her and fill her, had become an insistent drumbeat inside his body, but Marco knew that he could not give in to it. Not yet. Not until he had given Lily all the pleasure she deserved.

It was hard for him to go slowly and give her the time he thought she needed as he kissed his way down over her quivering stomach, following the path already taken by his hand which was now covering her sex. He stroked the soft mound with the pad of his thumb, and then when she gasped and moaned his name carefully caressed apart the neatly folded lips covering the swollen wet heat of her sex whilst he kissed the inner flesh of her thigh. He felt the shocked tremors of delight that ran through her.

Lily gasped in raw, agonised ecstasy. She couldn't bear it. She could not bear any more of the pleasure that was shooting through her in fiery waves, driving her higher and higher with every erotic touch of Marco's fingers and then his tongue-tip against the eager point of her desire. But even as she cried out her protest the dam broke, sending a series of pulsing quivers of release cascading over her.

Held fast in Marco's arms, Lily clung to him as the last surges of pleasure filled her. Her voice thick and soft with emotion, she whispered her gratitude to him. 'It was wonderful—everything I hoped for and more.'

Smoothing the damp hair back off her face, Marco smiled. 'That was just the beginning.' He loved her so much. Would always love her, he knew.

He kissed her slowly and deeply, taking time to rebuild her need until he was sure that her desire matched his own. Then he entered her slowly, carefully but firmly, stopping when he felt the shudder jolting through her.

But Lily shook her head and begged him fiercely, 'Don't stop. Please don't stop now, Marco. I want you so much. I want this so much.' She moved her body against his, gasping with pleasure when he responded, and she felt herself tightening around him, taking him, claiming him. The headiness of her own sense of wonder and triumph dazed her senses and filled her with erotic excitement.

She was all and everything he had been born for, Marco thought as he drove deeper and deeper into her, knowing she was moving with him, knowing that this time their journey was one they were sharing. Their discovery that their desire for one another, like their pleasure in one another, had no limits was a shared knowledge that had them exchanging kisses and touches and murmured words of praise and arousal until Marco felt his body tighten and surge and knew that he couldn't hold back. But even as the first pulse of his orgasm overtook him he felt Lily's flesh tighten round him, her cry of orgasmic relief mingling with his own.

Marco was still holding her close, his arms wrapped tightly around her. Hot tears scalded Lily's eyes. She had thought that knowing him like this would make her feel better, but instead it had made her feel worse. The tears spilled down onto her cheeks.

'You're crying. Why...?'

'Because I love you.'

The words had escaped before she could stop them, and now Marco was looking down at her, his own expression unreadable.

'I'm sorry,' she apologised. 'I know you don't want to hear that. I never meant to say it.'

Marco was holding her even more tightly, and his voice against her ear was raw with emotion as he murmured, 'You're wrong. I do want to hear it. There's nothing I've wanted to hear more than that my love for you is returned.'

Lily pulled back so that she could look into his eyes. What she could see in them told its own story, but still she had to whisper, 'You love me?'

And then she gasped with joy when Marco whispered back, between fiercely passionate kisses, 'Yes, yes—yes a thousand times. I love you and I always will. Lily, you've freed me from the prison I'd built round myself. You've shown me, taught me to trust in my emotions as well as to trust you. You've made me complete. You've healed me and made me whole. I love you for all those reasons, but more than that I love you because I cannot do anything else *but* love you. You stole my heart the first time I saw you, even though I didn't know it then. I fought against loving you. I tried to deny what was happening to me. I told myself that I would be a fool to let myself be controlled by my feelings. I told myself that I couldn't trust you.'

'Because of her? Because she hurt you so very badly?' Lily guessed, cupping his face in her hands and kissing him tenderly. 'I knew there must have been something—someone who had made you want to lock away your feelings.'

Marco removed one of her hands from his face and slowly kissed each finger.

'It wasn't Olivia's fault—not really. My parents were caring, but of the old school. Physical intimacy wasn't something they encouraged. Such behaviour wasn't something they considered princely. When my governess took me down from the nursery to see them before I went to bed I had to bow to my mother and shake hands with my father.'

Lily's soft, compassionate, 'Oh, you poor little boy!' was all the balm that childhood ache needed.

'My governess and my school taught me that emotions were something that had to be controlled, not given in to. As a future prince I must be in control of them, not the other way around. I learned that emotions were dangerous. They certainly made me feel awkward, and contemptuous of the weakness of that awkwardness whilst I was growing up. Looking back now, knowing how I feel about you, I can see so much more clearly why Olivia might have wanted to rebel against that upbringing—and hers was much the same as mine. I should have been kinder to her—more understanding. What made it worse was that the woman in charge of the model agency that had hired her pretended to be on my side. She assured me that Olivia would be safe, and because of what I believed to be my right to having my opinions treated as important I was stupid and arrogant enough not to even question that she might be lying to me—which she was.'

That still galled him, Lily could tell. And why not? It would gall any man of pride. Marco was a proud man, and in her opinion he had a right to that pride, she decided lovingly. There was more than injured pride in his voice, though—much more. There was also pain and regret and guilt, and it made Lily's heart ache for him.

'She procured young models for men under the guise of finding them work.'

'And that was why you thought what you did about me?'

'Yes,' Marco admitted. 'I told myself that you were two of a kind and kept on telling myself that—even when deep inside I knew you were nothing like her. But by then, of course, I had another and far more personal reason for not wanting to trust you. So I punished you for my mistakes and my own weakness. I misjudged you in so many different ways—over Pietro, over Anton—because I wanted and needed to misjudge you. It was easier and safer than acknowledging what I really felt about you. I thought I was being strong, but in reality I was being weak.'

'Not weak, Marco. You could never be weak. You were doing what you had taught yourself to do. What loving Olivia and losing her in such a terrible way had taught you to do,' Lily told him sympathetically.

Marco shook his head.

'No,' he said quietly. 'I didn't love her. At least not in the way that you mean. She was more like a sister to me than a future wife. I have only loved and will only love one woman, Lily, and that woman is you.'

He meant it, Lily could see.

'I was so afraid of loving you,' she admitted. 'I was afraid of being like my mother and loving a man who would only hurt me. And when you were so contemptuous of me, when you wouldn't believe me…'

'I hurt you,' Marco groaned, kissing her again. 'I hurt you because I was locked in a world where my emotions weren't allowed to exist. But you aroused them, and when you did I had to reject what you were making me feel. I had to tell myself that I couldn't trust you because I knew I couldn't trust myself to resist you.'

'But you saved me from Anton even though you didn't trust me.'

'You were so afraid. I couldn't turn my back on you.'

'And that is the man you really are, Marco. A man who can't turn his back on those in need even when he believes he has very good reason to reject them.'

'You give me credit where I don't deserve it.'

'No. You don't give yourself credit here, and you *do* deserve it.'

'I love you so much. So very much. I want you to marry me, Lily. I want us to be together for always. I want us to give our children—the children we shall create in our love for one another—the childhood that we never had.'

'Yes, I want that too,' Lily whispered beneath his kiss, as her senses and her body flowered into fresh eager longing beneath his touch.

EPILOGUE

THE final sound of the bells ringing out from the *castello's* chapel to announce their marriage were dying away, and the rose petals Lily had insisted on, instead of vulnerable doves being released, as their wedding planner had wanted were still drifting down from a perfect blue spring sky. The gentlest of breezes brushed the slender column of her wedding dress, its silk embossed with a traditional family design and especially made for her at the silk mill in Como in which Marco had an interest.

It had been a perfect day—but then every day since the day Marco had told her he loved her had been perfect in its own individual way.

'So many generations of your family have married and lived here,' Lily said as they stood arm in arm, watching their wedding guests.

'And hopefully many more will,' Marco told her, his hand resting deliberately against her body, where earlier that week the test Lily had done had confirmed their first child was already growing. A baby that would be born seven months into their marriage.

'I just hope we've done the right thing letting Rick take the photographs and video of the wedding,' she admitted to Marco, watching her half-brother photographing a group of pretty girls who were amongst the wedding guests.

Pietro, Marco's nephew, was assisting him. Once the misunderstanding over his modelling had been cleared up the two young men, so close in age, had become good friends, and were now work colleagues.

'It was very generous of you to fund the film Rick's going to make about the California wineries. His mother has told me that she intends to keep an eye on both him and Pietro whilst they are over there working on it.'

'Your brother is a good man at heart. But enough of family. I can't wait for us to leave for our honeymoon, so that I can have you to myself and show you and tell you how happy you've made me today, Lily. The happiest man in the world and the luckiest.'

'We've both been lucky,' Lily whispered back. 'Lucky to have found one another. Oh, Marco if we hadn't…'

'We had to,' Marco told her. 'We were destined to meet and love one another. Destined to be together, and we always will be.'

* * * * *

Mills & Boon® Large Print

October 2011

PASSION AND THE PRINCE
Penny Jordan

FOR DUTY'S SAKE
Lucy Monroe

ALESSANDRO'S PRIZE
Helen Bianchin

MR AND MISCHIEF
Kate Hewitt

HER DESERT PRINCE
Rebecca Winters

THE BOSS'S SURPRISE SON
Teresa Carpenter

ORDINARY GIRL IN A TIARA
Jessica Hart

TEMPTED BY TROUBLE
Liz Fielding

0911 Rom LP

Mills & Boon® Large Print

November 2011

THE MARRIAGE BETRAYAL
Lynne Graham

THE ICE PRINCE
Sandra Marton

DOUKAKIS'S APPRENTICE
Sarah Morgan

SURRENDER TO THE PAST
Carole Mortimer

HER OUTBACK COMMANDER
Margaret Way

A KISS TO SEAL THE DEAL
Nikki Logan

BABY ON THE RANCH
Susan Meier

GIRL IN A VINTAGE DRESS
Nicola Marsh

Mills & Boon® Online

Discover more romance at
www.millsandboon.co.uk

- ❧ **FREE** online reads
- ❧ **Books** up to one month before shops
- ❧ **Browse our books** before you buy

...and much more!

For exclusive competitions and instant updates:

 Like us on **facebook.com/romancehq**

 Follow us on **twitter.com/millsandboonuk**

 Join us on **community.millsandboon.co.uk**

Visit us Online   Sign up for our FREE eNewsletter at **www.millsandboon.co.uk**